In spite of herself, she'd had a good time.

Certainly, a hell of a lot better time than she'd had on her past half dozen dates combined. And…well, okay. Might as well admit it. She liked Mike. Really, truly liked him. He listened to what she had to say, and what *he* had to say was interesting to listen *to*. While he could be irreverent, which was fine, he was still a gentleman, which was better.

And there he was, not in the least bit interested in having a relationship. She'd finally met someone smart and nice and generous—attractive, even—and he was already married to his work.

Didn't that just beat all?

Dear Reader,

Chain letters! Don't you just hate them? Thanks to the joys of E-mail (and most of the time it really *is* a joy), I seem to receive them on pretty much a daily basis. The worst thing is, I keep getting the same ones over and over. No, I take that back. The worst thing really is that none of them ever come true. I'm still making ends meet but not getting rich, and I certainly haven't met Mr. Right. Luckily for Shayna Gunther, heroine of Robyn Amos's debut Yours Truly novel, *Bachelorette Blues,* her chain-letter experience has a happier outcome. She *does* meet her perfect match—though it takes her a little while to figure that out. (Just for the record: *I* would have recognized him a *lot* sooner!)

After you finish enjoying Shayna and Max's story, move on to the final installment of Karen Templeton's fabulous WEDDINGS, INC. trilogy. *Wedding? Impossible!* turns out not to be so impossible after all, of course. Admittedly, Zoe's a bit wary of her supposedly perfect blind date, Mike, but who wouldn't be? (If you say you wouldn't, you've never been on a blind-date disaster!) But pretty soon she's hooked, agreeing with everyone else's opinion of Mike—that he's wonderful—and planning that extremely possible wedding after all.

Enjoy! And remember to come back next month for two more books all about the fun of meeting—and marrying!—Mr. Right.

Yours,

Leslie J. Wainger
Executive Senior Editor

Please address questions and book requests to:
Silhouette Reader Service
U.S.: 3010 Walden Ave., P.O. Box 1325, Buffalo, NY 14269
Canadian: P.O. Box 609, Fort Erie, Ont. L2A 5X3

KAREN TEMPLETON

Wedding?
Impossible!

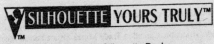

Published by Silhouette Books
America's Publisher of Contemporary Romance

This book is dedicated to anyone who's ever had to
balance career and home life and been able to survive
those times when it all comes crashing down
on your head; to my boys, who are still waiting for that
in-ground pool; and to Jack, as always

ACKNOWLEDGMENTS
To Paula Johnson and Tom Keith, for their invaluable
insights on the advertising business.
Any misapprehensions are mine, not theirs.

SILHOUETTE BOOKS

ISBN 0-373-52085-9

WEDDING? IMPOSSIBLE!

About the author

Choices. Women have more than ever these days. We may choose to be single or to marry, to have children or not, to have a career or not. It's not always easy to make the right decisions, especially when "having it all" can easily turn into "having more than we can handle." But with the right partner, and a lot of love, we *can* juggle all the balls and not get conked on the head. Well, at least not *too* often! In *Wedding? Impossible!* Zoe and Mike find themselves faced with unexpected choices— falling in love only makes their already frantic lives even more complicated. I can relate. But since I've seen how it can work in my own life, I have no qualms that they'll get it all figured out, as well. And, as they say, getting there is half the fun!

Writing is a natural outgrowth of my theater background, giving me the opportunity to direct, design and play all the parts—all without having to leave the house. A transplanted East Coast native, I now live in Albuquerque with my husband and four of my five sons (the oldest only recently left the nest). I love to hear from my readers, who may write to me c/o Silhouette Books, 300 East 42nd Street, Sixth Floor, New York, NY 10017.

Karen Templeton

Books by Karen Templeton

Silhouette Yours Truly

*Wedding Daze
*Wedding Belle
*Wedding? Impossible!

* Weddings, Inc.

1

The rain was the least of it.

And mind you, this was no ordinary rain. *This* was one of those umbrellas-were-worth-squat, even-your-bra-feels-wet deluges that led even the most unflappable mother to seriously consider the merits of Prozac and tranquilizer darts.

Still, Zoe Chan's grumpiness on this, her twenty-sixth birthday, couldn't be blamed on the weather. Or that she was being held hostage in a Chinese restaurant by two married sisters determined to make her life a living hell.

No. It was much more subtle than that. Much more worrisome.

For the past few days, she now realized, a niggling, spidery sort of thought had been scrabbling around in her brain trying to convince her that she wasn't, perhaps, quite as happy with her life as she thought she had been.

Now what, she wondered, was she supposed to do about that?

Chattering nonstop on the opposite side of the booth, her sisters seemed oblivious to her vexation. Thank God. Because if they had noticed and subsequently asked her what was wrong, she couldn't have told them. Well, that wasn't quite true. She could have told them *what* bothered her, at least at the moment. She just couldn't have told them *why.*

But the *what* list would probably have given them enough to chew on, anyway. Everything irritated her. The relentless twang of recorded Chinese music, the clatter of metal serving dishes and constantly clunking porcelain on bare Formica tabletops, a hundred yapping voices in the crowded restaurant, even the stupid screens with the stupid pandas prancing in fields of stupid bamboo—it was all driving her to distraction.

She stared at her plate, poking disinterestedly at a sliver of moo-shu pork that stubbornly refused to turn into a hamburger.

Unreasonably, her eyes stung. Criminy—she couldn't even have what she wanted for her lunch on *her* birthday. But this little luncheon had become sort of a "thing" among the three women, their births strung out over a scant three years. A Dog, a Pig and a Rat, according to the Chinese zodiac, which Vanessa—the most traditional of the three—swore by. There were worse combinations, heaven knew. And Zoe truly loved her sisters. So much so she couldn't find a way to tell them that, the Chinese blood in her veins notwithstanding, she hated Chinese food. Always had.

They would not have understood.

Any more than they would have understood there was another subject she'd just as soon see die a quick death.

"So…" Vanessa began, her blunt-cut black hair skirting the shoulders of her navy blazer as she expertly pinched a broccoli floret with her chopsticks. *Here it comes,* Zoe thought with an inward sigh. Her oldest sister had been married less than a year, which meant she was still, for all intents and purposes, in honeymoon mode. Bad news. "You seeing anyone these days?"

If she was smart, she'd lie. Make up someone, throw her sisters off the scent. And if she'd thought she had a worm's chance in a trout's stream of it working, she would have.

"No," she said in her best and-that's-all-you're-getting voice.

That might have been enough for the marginally more reticent Vanessa, but Margi's pregnancy-swollen middle made her far more dangerous. What was with pregnant women and their obsessive need to eradicate singlehood from the face of the earth?

"Why not?" Margi asked, shoveling in beef-fried rice as fast as she could get chopsticks from bowl to mouth.

With a shrug—the safest reply she could think of—Zoe stuck the bite of pork into her mouth. It still wasn't a hamburger.

Or fried chicken. Oh, man—she'd kill for KFC right about now.

She saw the exchanged glance, the shared sigh of concern. Baby Sister needed to be married, too. Baby Sister was missing out. Baby Sister...

Wished everyone would leave her the hell alone.

"It's just not right," her oldest sister started in, for at least the hundredth time since her own wedding, "that you should spend your entire life helping other women plan their weddings and not even be *dating*...ohmigod."

Zoe looked up, startled. She'd never heard the Vanessa say "ohmigod" in her life. Before she could assess this development, however, Vanessa reached across the table, snagging Zoe's hand so fast the shrimp she'd just captured with her chopsticks sailed across the table, barely missing Vanessa's teacup. "Catch the action in the back booth."

Catch the action...? Marriage was definitely having a strange effect on the woman.

Picking up her cue, Margi let loose with an appropriate but discreet gasp, before madly fanning herself with her left hand, her wedding set glinting in the subdued overhead lights of the restaurant. "Oh, Lordy, Lordy...there goes my blood pressure. Zo, you've *got* to check this guy out—"

"Why?"

Twin sets of onyx eyes glared at her in disbelief.

"Because he's *adorable*—"

"And?"

With a slight wince, Margi prodded her seventh-month load as she shook her head. "You are pitiful, you know that?" Her face collapsed into a frown for a second or two until the baby shifted, after which it lit up in a beatific—and deadly—smile.

"Here's this guy, who's like China's answer to Pierce Brosnan, back there—"

"All alone," Vanessa interjected, chomping the end off a spring roll.

"All alone," Margi echoed. "No discernible rings or girlfriends or wives or anything, and you mean to tell me your interest isn't even a *teensy* bit piqued?"

"Nope."

Her sisters sighed in heartfelt unison, glanced at each other again and went back to stuffing their faces.

Zoe knew the cease-fire wouldn't last. It never did.

And never would, not until they saw her enjoying the fruits from the same basket of conjugal bliss as they. And a Chan with a mission was not something to be taken lightly. Zoe should know.

But theirs was a pointless mission for two reasons. One, Zoe had her craw full of disastrous dates. And two, the days of her sisters trying to run her life were over. Even if she had agreed to have her birthday lunch in a Chinese restaurant. For the past year, since…Walter—she still shuddered at the mention of his name, even if she was one who mentioned it— she'd let them fix her up probably a dozen times, just to get them off her case. Even though every single one of their "finds" had been a dud. Or worse.

Not that the paltry few dates she'd managed to get on her own had been any better. She was beginning to wonder if she had a sign stamped across her forehead reading "If You're A Jerk, An Idiot Or A Pervert, Ask Me Out."

No matter. She gave her head a little shake, shivering as her waist-length hair tickled her through the flimsy—and damp—georgette of her 'thirties retro dress. This birthday, she decided, marked a change in her priorities: how she viewed life, what she wanted and expected from it.

Where once she assumed she'd eventually get married, now she wasn't even interested.

Where once not having a boyfriend had made her feel incomplete, now, she thought, perhaps she preferred the idea of being unentangled.

Where once she'd harbored hope that each new man she met might be "the one," now she no longer cared.

In other words—*no more men.*

She'd convinced herself—or, at least, was in the process of convincing herself—that this new attitude was remarkably freeing. Life was so much easier without a mess of expectations strangling it. Zoe Chan was going to be Proud and Single for the rest of her life, and damned if she wasn't going to enjoy it. If it killed her.

Needless to say, she had yet to share this news with the set of loving piranhas on the other side of the booth. Letting her family meddle in her life gave them a sense of purpose, she knew. Telling them to back off at this stage of the game would very likely cause hurt feelings. Zoe certainly didn't want that.

But she wanted their interference less.

Her peripheral vision caught a slight male form in a white short-sleeved shirt and black pants approaching the table.

"Ah…ladies. Everything okay here?"

Her sisters both flashed Colgate smiles at the white-haired man now standing beside them. David Wu was the proprietor of the Golden Dragon, an institution in the downtown Atlanta neighborhood for more than forty years, though Margi's pregnancy had only recently made her Mr. Wu's best customer. There was something so banal, Zoe reflected, about a pregnant Chinese woman craving Chinese food. Zoe was sure she would crave something else. Like souvlaki. Or lasagna.

But then, she reminded herself, as such a scenario was unlikely in her future, there was no point thinking about it.

"So, Mr. Wu…" Margi tucked one side of her chin-length hair behind her ear. "The guy sitting all alone back there… You know who he is?"

Subtle.

A maze of wrinkles swallowed up the old man's black eyes as he grinned. "My grandson," the diminutive man supplied. "Just got in from trip to New York little while ago. But why you ask, Missus Lee? You not exactly in market." He nodded toward her stomach, then laughed, a peculiar sound that reminded Zoe of a cat hacking up a fur ball.

"Oh..." Margi's eyes opened wide, all innocence. "I was just...curious."

That's all she needed to say. Mr. Wu's gaze drifted to Zoe. "Ah...yes..."

Zoe suddenly had to pee, not surprising after six cups of tea. Damn. Which meant she'd have to go to the back of the restaurant. Past Mr. Wu's grandson.

So what? she scolded herself. *The guy's just having his lunch, minding his own business. He has no idea who I am, or that, in my sisters' eyes, he's a marked man.*

"I'll be back in a sec." She flopped her napkin on the table as she slid out of the booth, rearranging her clammy, rumpled dress from where it had skootched around her hips. "Ladies' room," she added before either woman could say a word. When she turned around, however, the back booth was empty.

She refused to believe she was disappointed.

Mike crossed through the pristine kitchen to his grandfather's small, cluttered office to retrieve his suit jacket and briefcase. In spite of how full the restaurant was, there were only four cooks on duty at the moment. During the dinner rush, however, there could be as many as eight, more if his grandfather was hosting a wedding banquet. The past few years had seen a lot of turnover, Mike knew. Many of his grandfather's older employees had retired, and the younger people rarely stayed longer than six months. Things weren't the way they used to be, when a Chinese entrepreneur, once established in America, could import eager relatives from the mainland to help with the family business.

Not even his own progeny had followed in David Wu's footsteps, a fact the old man had accepted with better grace than most. Of the three children, the boys had become a lawyer and a CPA, and the girl—Mike's mother—a physician, all made possible by mountains of fried rice and spring rolls and the best shrimp sizzling rice soup this side of New York. As for the next generation, neither Mike nor any of his far-flung cousins had the slightest interest in going into the restaurant business.

Which had not diminished the old man's position as family patriarch one iota.

Mike glanced out the small high window in the office, noting it was still raining. Not as hard as before, but enough to still need his umbrella, which he retrieved from the metal wastebasket where he'd left it earlier, propping it against the front of the metal desk. As he stood poking through his briefcase, getting ready for his two o'clock appointment, he heard the double metal doors to the kitchen swing open, followed by a string of orders barked out in Chinese, a language Mike had never learned. To his ears, the harsh, nasal language could make anything—even relaying table five's menu choices— sound like a reprimand.

Immediately afterward, his grandfather burst into the office. At eighty-five, he still had the energy—and frequently the arrogance—of a young rooster. David Wu would give up the ghost before he gave up his business.

"Ladies in booth six, they want to meet you."

He slanted his grandfather a glance, then returned to studying the poorly done brochure in his hand. From a toy company, owned by an enterprising African-American woman who thought children should have the opportunity to play with action figures of various colors. Oh, yeah…a little spiffing up of the sales literature would do wonders—

"You hear me?"

Mike chuckled, slipped the brochure into his briefcase, clicked it shut. He'd heard. And, in spite of the dim lighting in the dining room, Mike had noticed the three young Chinese women in the booth across the aisle. Not that he was interested, even in theory. They were pretty, that's all. Sisters, he guessed—at least the two he could see—judging from the particular way both sets of eyebrows arched, the similarity of the unusually slim noses. However, he was sure he'd seen at least two sets of wedding diamonds at that booth.

But not, apparently, three, if his grandfather's hopeful expression meant anything.

With an unthreatened grin, Mike leaned against the back of his grandfather's desk and crossed his arms over his chest. "I heard you. You don't give up, old guy, do you?"

"Your parents not here to see you properly settled. The ladies, they tell me when youngest sister go to bathroom that she not married. You should meet. I know these people—good family, smart daughters." He leaned over and patted Mike on the upper arm. "The unmarried one, she prettiest of the three."

"Poppa, I appreciate your interest...but back off, okay?"

"What kind of expression is this...'back off'? This how you speak to venerable old grandfather?" The old man was teasing, his wide grin shoving several dozen wrinkles into new positions on his long, slender face.

"This is how I speak to venerable old grandfathers who stick their noses in where they don't belong."

"Not right, you still single. This way, you grow old with no children to support you, to respect you—"

"Or give you grief," Mike pointed out.

Mr. Wu waved away his objection, clucking his tongue. "You need wife. Life partner. Someone to share joy with. To make sorrow not so hard."

Mike huffed out a sigh. It would be easier, he supposed, if he didn't agree with his grandfather, at least on some level. But still... "Poppa—how many women have I dated in the last two years?"

Thin, delicately drawn eyebrows hitched up. "How I know that?"

"Okay, guess."

"Two? Three?"

"Eight."

"*Eight?*"

"Mmm-hmm. Longest relationship lasted three months."

The elderly man crossed his arms, his eyes narrowing to slits. "*Bu hao*—this not good thing."

Though probably not from the same standpoint, Mike agreed. "No."

"No matter. You just not meet right woman yet. Have to admit, harder for Monkey to find mate, maybe...but not impossible." He grinned. "My father, he Monkey, too. He married my mother when he thirty-six. Still they together more than fifty years." Wiry shoulders lifted in a shrug beneath his open-collared white shirt. "Sometimes just take a while."

Mike shrugged into his gray pinstriped jacket and picked up his briefcase, deciding that there was little point to be gained by discussing the merits—or lack thereof—of ancient folklore. Besides, it wasn't folklore that got in his way. It was life. *His* life.

"Pop," he said with the exasperation that comes with sudden realization, "I barely have time to date, let alone take care of a wife. Not the way I think a wife should be taken care of, anyway. I can't see marrying someone only to leave her home alone every night. And what if we had kids? The idea of absentee parenthood holds no appeal, believe me. I spend twelve, sixteen hours a day at work, am out of town more than I'm in...." He shook his head. "Marriage just wouldn't work for me.... What?"

His grandfather was giving him The Look.

"You talking to someone in restaurant business. Sixteen-hour days, seven days a week. And I was married. Your grandmother work right beside me, we very happy."

Mike ran a hand over his mouth. He remembered his mother's tales of his grandmother's constant exhaustion, how frustrated she had been with the task of helping Pop with the restaurant while raising three children. She had been devoted to her husband, loyal and uncomplaining and gracious. But far from happy, which his grandfather would have known had he taken two minutes to notice the weariness in his wife's eyes, according to Mike's mother. In fact, it was his grandmother's very discontent that had steered her children as far away from the business as they could get. And since Mike had made a bed similar to his grandfather's, he'd just have to sleep in it.

Alone.

As he had neither the time nor the energy for an argument, he decided to leave this where it lay. "I'll take that under advisement," he said, noncommittal. He tightened his grasp around the handle of his briefcase; when he lugged it off the desk, it seemed heavier than usual. "Gotta get to my appointment. I'll see you later—"

The old man snagged his arm with pipe-cleaner fingers. "So...you say hello to the ladies on your way out?"

Mike stopped, sighed. Acquiesced. "Sure. Why not?"

But when he went back out into the dining room, there were only two women in the booth. The two who were already married.

His loud sigh of relief surprised even him.

Zoe vigorously shook out her umbrella before backing through the heavy front door into the salon. Grimacing, she dropped it into the brass stand in the vestibule like it was a dead mole, then ducked into the little powder room under the stairs to dry her hands and run a comb through her damp, wind-tangled hair.

Her sisters had done everything but tie her up, trying to keep her in the booth until Mr. Wu's grandson appeared, but Zoe pleaded an appointment she *had* to get back for and wriggled out of their grasp. Again.

There had been no appointment. In fact, things had been slower than frozen molasses at the bridal salon for the past week. Not unusual for September, though. Most Atlanta weddings were still held in the late spring, then remained steady through the summer months. But fall always brought a welcome reprieve. They'd get a spate of appointments for holiday weddings, after which the pace would pick up again around Christmas, when all the brides-to-be who'd received engagement rings as Christmas presents would start trickling in to begin planning their spring weddings. And so it went, year after year, the human mating cycle no less predictable than that of any other animal.

Today, however, was blissfully quiet, partially due to the relentless rain, Zoe supposed, although that appeared to be lightening up from what it had been this morning. The assistant manager had a doctor's appointment, and Zoe had given two of the consultants the afternoon off, as well, since both were slated to work Saturday weddings. Madge, the third saleswoman, was in the large corner fitting room with—Zoe checked the appointment book as she passed the reception area—Mitzi Stein. Oh, right. The redhead. Five-eight, killer boobs—which, to the slightly endowed Zoe, constituted anything larger than a B cup—a temple wedding in November, eight bridesmaids, custom-designed wedding gown.

On automatic pilot, Zoe wandered around the waiting room, picking up a stray bridesmaid gown here, a coffee cup there, straightening out the stacks of *Modern Bride* on the marble-topped table between the pair of matching peach velvet Victorian love seats. An occasional burst of raucous laughter from one of the three full-time seamstresses filtered through the muffled whirr of sewing machines from the alteration workshop in the back of the building. Nice to hear *somebody* was happy.

Suddenly weary, she dropped onto one of a half-dozen pale lemon club chairs scattered throughout the large room, the magazines clutched to her chest. Then she sighed. Loudly.

She was, she decided, suffering from a walloping case of bridal burnout.

Yesterday, she had thought this room perfect. And somewhere underneath her funk, she supposed it still was. The original front parlor and formal dining room in the century-old Queen Anne had been combined into one room probably forty years earlier by Luella Martin, from whom Brianna Fairchild had bought both the bridal business and the house five years ago. Gone was the horrid Pepto-Bismol pink decor—Luella's Legacy, they had not so fondly dubbed it. Now the walls were a soft Wedgwood green, the half-dozen multipaned windows swagged in a delicate multicolored English chintz. The glow from several crystal lamps diffused the velvety light filtering through ivory lace panels Brianna had brought back from a trip to Ireland a year ago. The antique love seats happily mingled with the contemporary club chairs, and Zoe herself had picked out the white wicker armchairs cushioned in sherbet-striped canvas. Tying all the colors together was an enormous Aubusson rug that Brianna's mother-in-law had found rolled up in her attic. As an extra touch, lush bouquets of late roses and chrysanthemums from Brianna's own garden spilled from an assortment of milk-white vases scattered throughout the room.

Zoe sighed again, feeling no less burdened after the rush of air had left her lungs. It was "touches" like this that made Fairchild Bridals the choice for many of Atlanta's socialite brides, that made Zoe proud to work for the talented, bright woman who'd made this business what it was. She'd still been in college when she'd taken the job as Brianna's assistant four years ago; then, after graduation, her employer—newly married and pregnant—had promoted her to full manager.

It had been a good job, if hectic at times. Zoe was well paid, and one of the perks was a large, airy apartment over the Inwood Park salon that had been Brianna's before her marriage. Now her boss lived in north Buckhead with her husband, two small children and her delightful Auntie Mame of a mother-in-law, only coming into the salon a few times a week.

Which, as Brianna so often reminded Zoe, was only possible because she could rely on Zoe to handle things as carefully as she would handle them herself.

The rain had picked up again, drumming against the wrap-around porch roof. Frowning, Zoe hauled herself out of the chair, for a not-so-brief moment tempted to walk back out the door and keep walking, rain or no rain. If she'd had the slightest clue where she might walk *to,* she might have done just that. Instead, being the reliable, trustworthy, loyal creature she was, she returned instead to the office to take care of some paperwork. After all, work was the perfect antidote to self-pity, her grandmother had always said. And, God knew, there was enough to do around here to keep her from thinking about herself until she was so shriveled up, she wouldn't be able to get excited about a man if one dropped out of the sky at her feet.

She veered around her office door, startled to find Brianna whizzing around the office tacking sketches to bulletin boards and muttering to herself. Although the blonde had pulled back her shoulder-length hair into a bowed silk scarf at the nape of her neck, she periodically swiped at several strands that had worked their way loose and were floating about her face. An oversize apricot silk shirt—with the sleeves characteristically rolled up to her elbows—and matching baggy pants all but swallowed up her long, thin figure. Also typical, she had discarded her shoes somewhere along the way.

"Brianna! What are you doing here—?"

"Zo!" Brianna reached her in two strides, grabbing her by the shoulders. Even shoeless, she stood a good eight inches taller than Zoe. "I got the Pierre!" she cried, her pale green eyes glittering with excitement. "The freakin' *Pierre!* You remember the room from the web site? The Regency, the one all in blues? It holds a hundred fifty people, if we do regular seating, which should be perfect for the major show. Then we can have them put cozy little tables back in for buying appointments." She let go of Zoe's shoulders and planted slim hands on slimmer hips. "And Spencer said I'd never be able to get it at this late date! Hah! Guess I showed him!"

Zoe couldn't ever remember seeing Brianna this wound up. Wishing the enthusiasm was contagious, she managed a half-hearted "That's terrific—"

"Oh! And I forgot to tell you—I gave an interview to the *Constitution-Journal*'s business editor for Sunday's paper." Brianna's laughter was soft and breathy as she clasped her hands in front of her, looking far younger than her thirty-six years. "It's taken a year, but I think it's just really sinking in, Zo—I'm going national!" Then she gestured toward the sketches tacked up all over the spacious room that Zoe still considered Brianna's office, even though Zoe had used the larger desk for three years. "I need to choose six more styles to make up the line. Which ones do you think would be best? Twenty is more than enough for starters, don't you think?"

What do you think? Don't you think...? What would be best, Zo?

Zoe did exactly as was requested, exactly what was expected of her, being what she had been to Brianna for four years—her sounding board, her right hand, her auxiliary brain. And for four years, she had reveled in her position, using her keen sense of style, her organizational skills, her attention to detail to win her employer's generous and heartfelt appreciation.

That vague, can't-put-a-finger-on-it malaise billowed and rose in her throat, threatening to choke her. As she studied the exquisite renderings of bridal gowns that other women would try on, buy, be married in, she found herself blinking, again and again, with the effort not to cry.

She took a deep breath, swallowed. Oh, *yuck*—this self-pity business was for the birds. What happened to all the stuff she'd told herself in the restaurant? She didn't need men in her life. They were just an unnecessary complication. It was okay to be single, despite her family's harping. Getting teary about this was just...dumb.

The sketches blurred.

Brianna came up behind her. "I thought we should probably keep most of the line in the middle range, maybe a half-dozen lower-priced ones in order to get some mass production going, and keep a handful of the pricier gowns for the stores that want an exclusive... Hey, Zo." Zoe felt a gentle touch on her shoulder. "Honey...are you crying?"

Right on cue, two tears escaped and dribbled down Zoe's cheeks. "No," she said.

Brianna held out one hand, palm up, lifting her eyes to the ceiling. "Nope. No leaks." Then she looked at Zoe again. "So that's not rain I see on your cheeks, missy."

Zoe tried to laugh, but that only unleashed the tears. She could have spit, she was so ticked off.

"Oh, jeez…come here." Brianna slipped a slender arm around Zoe's shoulders and led her over to a padded bench along one wall, sitting her down. She snatched a tissue out of the boutique box on a nearby table, handed it to her. "Okay—what's all this about?"

"Nothing." She blew her nose.

"Yeah, right. Talk to me, Zo."

Zoe screwed up her mouth. "Nothing to talk about."

"Honey…" Brianna took Zoe's hands in hers, her softly accented voice washing over her assistant's frayed nerves. "Listen, kiddo, we've been friends for a long time. When I went through all that mess with the baby and Spencer three years ago, you were right there for me. I'd like to think you'd let me return the favor." She tried to get Zoe to look at her. "If I can?"

With a shrug, Zoe said, "And if I knew what was going on, I'd probably let you." She glanced up at Brianna's smooth, calm face. A contented face, she realized. The same expression her sisters wore. And her mother. The expression women wore when they had just what they wanted, when they knew they were loved.

Tears pricked again at Zoe's eyes, and she quickly looked away.

She was *not* envious of her employer. Or her sisters. She didn't need a man to be happy. She didn't need romantic love to feel validated as a woman, as a human being. And she certainly didn't need her sisters, or anyone else, to tell her that she did.

Then why was she so miserable? And she was miserable. Not just blue, or moody, or cranky. But bawl-her-eyes-out *wretched*.

She really, *really* hated feeling like this.

"What did you feel…?" she began, then shook her head and started over. "Before you met Spencer, did you think you were happy?"

Brianna backed up slightly, her golden brows hitching up. "What a funny thing to ask," she said gently. "I guess I pretty much just took things as they came. Kept busy, refused to think about it. Although…" Her lips tugged into something resembling a grimace. "I was very lonely at times." She snorted. "Which is what eventually got me into trouble."

Zoe nodded, remembering all too clearly the shock of discovering that her cool, collected boss had become pregnant, courtesy of a one-time lapse of judgment. Brianna's daughter, Melissa, was not her husband's biological child, although she was being raised—and adored—as his. Although things had worked out in almost fairy-tale style for the lovely woman sitting next to her, her experience had served as an all-too-clear reminder of situations to avoid.

As if she'd heard Zoe's thoughts, Brianna added, "But you assured me at the time that you were wise enough to avoid that particular trap." She hesitated, then carefully asked, "You have, haven't you? Avoided that particular trap?"

Zoe offered her a perplexed half shake of her head.

"Is this…about a man?" Brianna prompted.

"Oh! Lord, no," Zoe breathed out, then tucked her arms tightly against her chest. "No, there's no man." She imbued her words with as much finality as she could muster. "It's just…a mood, I suppose. It'll pass."

One thing Zoe admired about Brianna was her ability to tell when to back off. Her employer squeezed her shoulders, then asked, as if the previous conversation had never occurred, "So…about these designs. Tell me which are your favorites."

It was ridiculous, Zoe chastised herself, getting so worked up about absolutely nothing. She had a wonderful job, a great boss, a family who was always there for her—even if its members were often a little more *there* than she might have liked. She was healthy, she could come and go as she pleased, her income was sufficient to allow her to buy a new outfit or indulge in an expensive dessert without feeling guilty. She rarely even had bad hair days.

What else did she need?

Dutifully Zoe rose from the bench and walked back over to look at the sketches. And did, as she had done for her entire life, as she was asked.

Whining, she sternly reminded herself, was for wusses.

Since it was so quiet, Zoe closed the salon at five, sending everyone home and forwarding the salon's calls to her personal phone upstairs. She indulged in a long soak in the old claw-footed tub, then put on a black jersey jumpsuit in anticipation of going to her parents' for her birthday dinner.

An event she seriously doubted would lift her mood.

The afternoon had passed uneventfully enough, she supposed. They'd decided on the rest of the line, after which Brianna had left to meet with her accountant and banker. Zoe had then spent an hour or more on the phone wrangling with assorted fabric and lace and trim vendors in New York. By four o'clock, she had accumulated a nice stack of faxes confirming quantity pricing and availability so there wouldn't be any problems once they went into mass production. At least she'd had no hassles about credit—in five years of business, Brianna had never paid a bill a minute past its due date. And Zoe had to admire her boss for sticking to her guns about refusing to use her husband's name or money as a stepping stone to her own success.

Zoe had learned a great deal from Brianna. And she owed her a great deal, as well. She knew she had it better, jobwise, than a lot of other college grads out there. Whatever this dissatisfaction was, it had to be temporary. She couldn't leave Brianna, especially now when she was about to launch her new line. Zoe simply didn't do things that way. Besides—what else would she do?

Chewing over this surprising thought, she slipped on her black angora cardigan and grabbed her purse. But the second her hand lit on the doorknob, the phone rang. She hesitated, then thought it might be one of the forwarded calls.

It wasn't.

"Zoe?" Her mother's tentative voice floated over the wire. "Yeah, Ma. I was just—"

"Got a minute?"

Zoe glanced at the mantel clock. Yep. After six. "Did I get the dates mixed up, or am I not going to be seeing you, in person, in less than a half hour?"

"Margi tells me she and Vanessa met David Wu's grandson today and they thought he'd be perfect for you."

Why beat *around* the bush when you can whop the sucker dead-on? was Susan Chan's motto.

"Ma..."

"Margi said he was adorable—"

What's worse than two married matchmaking sisters? Their mother.

"That's nice. Oh, Ma—I forgot to tell you! Guess who came into the salon yesterday—?"

"And has his own business—"

"Brittany Wang! Did you know she'd gotten engaged to Sam Cheung?"

"And not married—"

"And she picked out the most beautiful gown...."

When there was no response, Zoe prodded—tentatively, like one might poke a dead bug to make sure it really was dead. "Ma?"

"The only wedding dress I care to hear about anybody picking out," came the terse response on the other end of the line, "is your own. But I guess that's not going to happen. Margi said you wouldn't even *meet* the man."

Why, Zoe wondered, did mothers take everything as a personal insult?

"I couldn't," she replied flatly. "I had an appointment."

"A few minutes wouldn't have killed you."

"Ma, please—not now, okay?"

"Not now, not ever, the way you're going. When was the last time you even went out?"

Zoe sighed. "What would you like me to do? Stand on the street corner and flag 'em down? Wear a sandwich board, maybe, advertising my availability?"

"Don't be smart, young lady."

"Well, for Pete's sake—"

"I just don't understand it, Zoe," her mother said on a sigh. "You're bright, intelligent, attractive, have a good sense of humor—"

"And there's no insanity in the family. At least not that we know of. Yeah, yeah, I know—I'm a perfect catch. Just ask Walter."

"Walter was not worthy of you…"

Couldn't disagree there.

"But not every man is like Walter."

At this point, she suddenly realized she was, in some fashion, having a fight with her mother. She *never* fought with her mother. In fact, while her sisters had each gone through a rebellious period in their teens, arguing with their mother about everything from hair to makeup to music, Zoe hadn't. Oh, she'd dressed a little eccentrically, perhaps, and had a smart mouth. But getting straight *A*s and never breaking curfew went a long way, she'd discovered, toward keeping parents at bay. She'd been the Perfect Daughter. And had, for the most part, enjoyed her rarefied status.

Until today.

"Ma, give it up, okay? And call off your dogs, too, while you're at it. Being single isn't a curse. Or a socially unacceptable disease. Maybe I'm not going to get married. Maybe I'm not meant to."

"Nonsense," her mother huffed. "You just have to keep trying."

"I don't want to keep trying!" Zoe slammed her hand against the wall next to the phone. Silently wincing and trying to shake out the sting, she continued. "I'm tired of going on blind dates and having to spend the entire evening slapping a guy's hands, or listening to some self-absorbed twiddlebug yammer endlessly about selling…whatever it is that particular twiddlebug sells, or defending my right as a woman to have an *opinion*, let alone a *career*, or trying to ignore some guy's disgusting postnasal drip. I have been groped, grossed out, patronized and bored as often as I care to be in one lifetime, thank you very much.''

After a pause, her mother said, "So maybe this guy is different.''

Zoe slapped her palm against her forehead and shook her head.

"The only way this guy could possibly be different," she finally said, "is if he was spawned of alien parents. Because I'm here to tell you, if he's human, he ain't different.''

"Now, Zoe...you're overreacting.''

Yeah, she was. And it felt good. And she didn't care. And she was going to continue to overreact until whatever this was that was threatening to make her crazy went away. Going to this party tonight, getting anywhere near her sisters and her mother, would be an exercise in masochism. So why go? It was *her* birthday, dammit, and all she wanted was to be by herself and not have to listen to well-meaning relatives tell her what they thought she needed.

So she straightened up, snuggled the phone more tightly against her ear and told her mother she suddenly didn't feel well and wouldn't be able to come to dinner after all. Then, before the stunned woman could say another word, Zoe apologized for messing up her mother's plans, told her she loved her, and hung up.

As Zoe changed out of her jumpsuit and threw on a pair of shorts and a sweatshirt, she heard the phone ring. As she traipsed into the kitchen, she heard the answering machine click on. As she grabbed the container of Häagen-Dazs Chocolate Chocolate Chip out of the freezer, she heard her mother's entreaty to pick up the phone so they could finish their conversation because she knew good and *well* there was nothing physically wrong with her, and if she hadn't been able to pull the wool over her eyes when she was a little girl, what on earth made her think she could get away with it now?

But she just had, hadn't she?

Zoe flopped down on the cinnamon velveteen sofa that Brianna had left behind after her marriage, shoveled an indelicate spoonful of ice cream into her mouth and quietly considered the prospect of consigning all men—well, the majority of them, anyway—to hell. And all relatives who tried to fix her up with those men could go along for the ride.

And if it weren't for the lump in her throat that kept the ice cream from sliding down as easily as it should, that thought might have given her some small sense of satisfaction. Because it had finally occurred to her—though why it had taken this long for her to remember, she didn't know—that a year ago today, she'd told Walter Yang she loved him. Which led to a confession from the man she'd been seeing, in every sense of the word, for more than six months, that while he was immensely flattered and thought Zoe was great and all that, well, see…he'd been dating other women. And fully intended to keep doing so.

All her life, Zoe had done what was expected of her, what she felt would make other people like her. Accept her. So she'd slept with Walter, because he asked her and because, for the first time, she cared enough about a man to want to make him happy. And, to be fair, she'd gotten her fair share of jollies, too.

But look where it had gotten her. Not pregnant, at least, but certainly no less embarrassed by her own idiocy.

She stared dejectedly at the ice cream softening so perfectly around the edges, then got up and went back to the kitchen, clamping the lid back on and shoving the container back into the freezer.

Slumping up against the refrigerator door, she shut her eyes. There were no tears, oddly enough. Just sort of a numbness, achy around the edges. The kicker, though, was the realization that, in that year between birthdays, nothing had changed. Maybe she was a little wiser and a lot more wary, but other than that…what strides had Zoe Chan made in the progress department? She still had the same job, same apartment, same weekly dinners with her parents. All around her, everyone else was moving forward, doing new things, witnessing changes— new jobs or careers, new husbands or children.

While she just spun her wheels.

Enough of this. She pushed herself away from the refrigerator and walked over to the window above the sink, scanning the backyard, her hands rammed into her shorts pockets. No matter what her mood, wallowing wasn't her style. There would still be daylight for a half hour or so. And it had finally stopped raining. She supposed she could go putz around in the garden for a while. Brianna hadn't actually said anything the last time she really noticed the flower beds, but Zoe could tell it tore at the woman's heart to see her once carefully tended garden die a slow, torturous death under Zoe's black thumb. Zoe was the only person, as far as she knew, who could kill Virginia creeper. If she put her mind to it, she could probably kill kudzu.

"Look at it this way," she muttered to herself as she dragged a pair of gardening gloves and some clippers out of the kitchen drawer. "How much crankier can I get?"

She should have known.

2

Sometimes, running was the only thing that worked.

Mike welcomed each jolt as his Adidas running shoes slammed again and again and again into the wet pavement. As he'd intended, he'd become oblivious to everything save the relentless, pistonlike rhythm of his thighs and each ragged gasp of air as he pushed through the thick silence of the drizzly evening. He swiped his hair off his forehead with the back of his wrist, enjoying the perversely pleasant clamminess of rain and sweat sheathing his skin.

For the past hour, he'd let his mind go numb, figuring that was healthier than indulging in irritation. Now, however, as the lactic acid began to build up in his muscles, so did some semblance of rational thought seep into his brain. If he had any sense, he'd head back.

As soon as he figured out where back was in relation to where he was.

Damned if he wasn't lost.

Another swipe at his forehead brought a soft snort. Thirty years old, head of his own thriving ad agency, familiar with a dozen major cities around the world, and he'd managed to get lost right here in Atlanta. Brilliant.

He slowed down at an intersection, running in place to keep his muscles from freezing up while he tried to get his bearings. The drizzle was nothing more than a light mist now, although pewter clouds still tumbled ominously overhead. Obviously, he was in Inman Heights, judging from the preponderance of rejuvenated Painted Ladies. A sedate area, unlike his hopping Little Five Points neighborhood. So sedate, in fact, that a female of indeterminate age, squatting by some flower beds in front of the graceful, corner-lotted Queen Anne directly across the street, was the only other human in sight.

Mike loped over to the house, slowing to a walk as he approached the young—he could tell that much now—woman. Out of the corner of his eye, he noticed a wooden framed sign of some sort on the front lawn.

She faced away from him, a curtain of shiny sable hair spilling down her back as she poked at some listless-looking plants. Her dusty blue sweatshirt was large enough to fit another girl or two inside, the shoulder seams nearly meeting the pushed-up cuffs, bunching the sleeves into a pair of soft accordions on her forearms. Bare legs, bordered by a mere inch of white shorts and ending in a pair of smudged sneakers, jutted out from underneath the shirt. Her agitated movements seemed to indicate she was in distress, although what sort of distress a chrysanthemum bush might cause, he had no idea.

"Don't you dare die!" Her hands jabbed into what he surmised were petite hips underneath the voluminous sweatshirt, causing her to wobble for a moment in the awkward position. "Mums are supposed to be foolproof. The lady at the nursery even said so. So you can't die! Do you hear me?"

"Excuse me...."

The young woman let out a tiny squeak before she toppled over, landing with a soft *thud* on her rear end in the damp grass. Like a bug trying to right itself, she clumsily got to her feet, a blush tingeing her delicate complexion. Obsidian eyes, duplicates of his own, nailed him from underneath wispy black bangs as she brushed off her bottom.

"What's the big idea, sneaking up on someone like that? You scared the..." She stopped, blinked twice, then said, "You scared me half to death." He saw a slight, but unmistakable grimace of disgust at his grungy state, and didn't blame her. He had the distinct—*very* distinct—impression he smelled like a wet dog.

Unfortunately.

He took a step back. "I'm really sorry. Are you all right?"

After a moment, she nodded. "Yeah, I'll live." Despite her obvious Chinese heritage, her speech was as thoroughly Americanized as his. His guess was third, maybe fourth generation. "What did you want?"

He wasn't sure anymore. Her edginess took him by surprise. Not because it was an unexpected reaction on her part, but because of the unexpected reaction on *his*.

He was interested. In her. In finding out what went on behind those suspicious eyes—who she was, what she did.

How she kissed.

Whoa.

"I'm lost," he said, and realized just how much.

The young woman rolled her eyes, then gave a wry laugh. "Yeah, right—"

"No, really, I am. I live over in Five Points and…" Mike took a sharp, short breath, let it out. Nothing to be done for it now. "And…I started running an hour ago and didn't…keep track of where I was going."

She pushed a hank of hair behind one tiny ear studded with a series of three gold balls. Almost in slow motion, her hand knuckled into her hip. Tilting her head, those bright eyes glistening in the hazy light, she allowed a cautious "Are you serious?" And her mouth twitched. Just for a microsecond, but he saw it.

"Believe me," he said, forking his hand through wet hair barely contained by his sweatband. "I can come up with better pick-up lines than that."

Instantly the sparkle of humor became a flash of anger. To be sure, it was subtle. But Mike had long since learned to tell the difference.

"I'll just bet you can," she muttered as she walked past him toward the curb, dusting dirt off her hands. He doubted she topped five feet, but everything—or what the sack of a sweatshirt let him see—was perfectly proportioned. He caught a whiff of her perfume, something light and spicy, and found himself liking the idea that she bothered to wear perfume to muck about in the garden.

Of course, he reminded himself as he glanced back at the house, he had no idea who she might have put the perfume on *for.* Or where that person might be. Probably in the house somewhere, reading the paper or washing the dinner dishes, waiting for her to return. Would he greet her with a sly smile, pull her into his arms, plant kisses along that smooth, ivory neck? Or would she grab a towel and start drying the dishes, telling him all about the crazy guy she'd just seen who'd gotten himself lost?

She might even have a kid. Maybe more than one.

With his luck.

She pointed to the left, her small hand weighted down with at least four silver rings—was one of them a wedding ring?—then promptly rattled off several street names, interspersed with appropriate "Turn lefts" and "Go down three blocks" and "Veer around the park until you get to…"

He hadn't heard a word she'd said.

"I…" He tried a smile. "I don't suppose you could write those directions down for me?"

She didn't even try to hide her sigh of annoyance. Still, she allowed a "Oh, all right. I'll be right back," before returning to the house. Soundlessly she ran up the stairs and disappeared inside. That she hadn't invited him in was not lost on him. That she'd been smart enough *not* to wasn't lost on him, either.

Of course, if she lived with some hunk with biceps the size of basketballs, staying outside was probably the wiser choice.

If *he'd* been smart enough to tuck some cash in his shorts pocket, he could have taken a cab home. Now he'd have to run back. Or walk, which would take even longer.

No matter. He could use the time to think about the Lowell account, since he had a meeting with the young software designer on Tuesday anyway.

If he could. Think about anything else, that is.

The annoyance left over from lunchtime came roaring back. His grandfather was out for blood. Preferably Mike's, in a marriage license blood test. The man hadn't given up in his "encouragement" that Mike ask out this Zoe Chan. "She perfect for you," David Wu had insisted when he'd called, catching Mike on the phone the minute he'd gotten home from work.

Yeah. Like all the other "perfect" women he'd dated the last couple of years. Actually, some of them were, he supposed. Just not for him.

"Just bring her here, to restaurant," his grandfather had said. "No big deal."

"Oh, right," Mike had replied. "No big deal. Except for the small point of your breathing down our necks while we ate. And I suppose her sisters would probably be there, too, a discreet two booths away, watching our every move. Forget it, Pop. What little private life I have, I'll keep private, thank you very much."

"So don't eat here. What do I care?" Then he'd changed his tack. "You always say, not one to let opportunity pass you by. This perfect opportunity."

And Mike had simply sighed and tried to explain that he had been talking about *business* opportunities. People, he'd said, were not opportunities.

Not unless they were potential accounts, anyway.

Business, he was good at. Great at. Women were something else again. Women, he simply couldn't seem to connect with. Of course, not many women were interested in connecting with someone who broke/rearranged/showed up late for as many dates as he did.

Had the old man not heard a word Mike said earlier that afternoon?

Behind him, a door slammed shut. He turned to watch the young woman skip down the porch steps and approach him, her full mouth now pulled into a tight, unrelenting line. Like a wisp of smoke, an odd, nagging thought winnowed through his brain that, just maybe, he could connect with this spunky little thing. Would sure like the chance to try, anyway. Passion and energy surged from this woman in waves of tsunami proportions.

Then she slapped the piece of paper with the directions written on it into his hand, and the thought evaporated.

"These should get you home." She whirled around and headed back to the chrysanthemums.

"Hey!" he called, watching the bottom of the sweatshirt sway in front of him. "Do you have a name?"

"Nope," she called back without bothering to glance over her shoulder.

She, obviously, was not the least bit interested in connecting with him. In any way, shape, form or fashion.

Damn.

Of all the male characteristics that annoyed Zoe, *charming* headed the list. Charming was a smoke screen, she had decided many years ago, for self-centered. Devious. Manipulative. *Walter* had been charming. To the bitter end, the creep could sweet-talk her into anything. Out of anything, too, as it happened. And the guy she'd just seen was one of the most charming men she'd ever met.

She jabbed the trowel into the dirt and sat back on her haunches.

Wasn't he, though?

She allowed a furtive glance over her shoulder, but of course he'd long since gone.

Wow. Soft black hair, just the right length. Strong, proud cheekbones in perfect proportion to an iron jaw—she sighed—with the most delectable cleft in his chin. Tall enough to be taken seriously, muscles in all the right places in just the right amount—enough to whet the appetite, but not overwhelming. And his voice, half growl, half purr...

Delicious.

She returned to loosening the packed soil around the struggling plant as if she thought there was buried treasure underneath it.

Testosterone alert! she reminded herself. Men were not on

her list anymore, remember? Any of them. She'd dated *charming* before. Not to mention perfect hair and shoulders and even tall, sometimes. There might even have been a cleft chin or two in the mix. Of course, none of her previous dates—translation: *disasters*—had combined all those yummy things in one package. Not even Walter.

She startled herself with her own laugh in the evening stillness.

Which only meant the potential for disaster would be all that much greater, right?

Right?

She looked over her shoulder again. And sighed.

Damn.

Mike dumped the business section of the Sunday paper on his office manager's desk before the glass office door had fully swept to a close behind him.

"Our next client, Fran."

"'Good morning, Fran. How was your weekend?'" she prompted, not looking up from opening the mail.

"Good morning, Fran. And how was your weekend?"

"Lovely, dear, thanks for asking." Now the pudgy, sweet-faced woman peered over her reading glasses at the paper. "General Motors? Aren't we being a little ambitious, Michael?"

"Cute, Frannie. No—the bridal gown lady. Brianna Whatsername."

The redhead picked up the paper to get a better look, handing Mike a wad of messages as she did. "Oh…*her*. Oh, my, yes," she said on an appreciative breath. "I've been to a couple of weddings where she designed the gowns. They were stunning…yes…" Her voice trailed off as she read. "So she's designing a full-fledged line. And her first showing is in New York next month—"

"I read the article, Fran," Mike said mildly as he dropped into one of the cubelike red armchairs in the waiting area, sorting the messages by order of urgency.

"Well, I haven't, so just shut up for two seconds," the woman shot back, swatting in his general direction as she continued to read. Then, finished, she steadily regarded him over her glasses. "Did she call you?"

"Nope." Mike grinned, unperturbed. He got up, crossed over to a poster of the Sparkling Pure Water ad that had appeared in all the MARTA stations last year, straightened it against the charcoal wall. "We're contacting *her*."

His assistant's mouth pulled tight. "Why?"

"Because she's loaded, Fran. And, from what I can tell, she has a good product."

"Then, since you've already read the article, hotshot, I assume you noticed the part where she said she didn't think a lot of advertising was necessary, since she felt she was already somewhat known in the business?"

"Mmm-hmm."

"Which was like waving a red flag in front of you, wasn't it?"

"Ah, Frannie, my love…you know me too well."

"That's what worries me," the woman muttered, returning her attention to the page in front of her. As she read, she absently tugged at the top button of her gray cardigan.

"Oh, come on," Mike said, easing a hip onto the front of her desk. "You have to get the big picture. The woman's married to one of the richest men in the country—whose money, she took great pains to point out, she's not using. Or at least she says she's not. But the fact remains we're talking celebrity socialite here. Look at that photo—the woman radiates elegance. This is the first new major bridal house to appear in years, right when weddings—*big* weddings—are more popular than ever."

His assistant's hazel eyes widened. "And how do we know this, Mr. Sooner Dead-than-Wed?"

He ignored the gibe. "Big article on the Internet the other day. Anyway, I picture these gowns in *Vogue,* not just *Bride's.* A spread in *Town and Country,* maybe. No, definitely."

Fran cocked her head. "Not cheap ads."

"True."

"Which would mean a good commission."

"True again."

"But if she says she doesn't want to spend a lot on advertising—"

Mike grinned. "She'll change her mind, believe me. As soon as she sees the ad campaign I'm working up even as we speak." He tapped his head. "In here."

"So…I suppose this means I should give her a call?"

He plopped a kiss on top of Fran's gingery waves. "That's what I love about you, Fran. Always one step ahead of me."

"Purely self-preservation," Mike heard her mumble over the *thunk* of the Yellow Pages hitting her desk as he went into his office.

It wasn't a large office, or posh, but the address was fairly decent and the view was magnificent. Nor was he, as Fran so backhandedly pointed out, ready to handle accounts large enough to advertise during the Super Bowl. But he was getting there, in his own way, on his own terms, and to everyone's benefit.

Mike took care of his accounts, personally and carefully. His specialty was small, stable companies with a terrific product that needed a little push to give them that extra foothold in the marketplace. Much of his billing was below industry standard, although, to date, every one of the companies he'd helped get a leg up had repaid him, either by increasing their advertising budget or in referrals.

But…he needed the occasional plum account to subsidize the little guys. He wouldn't deny he saw Fairchild Bridals as a potential gold mine, especially if he could talk its lovely owner into tapping into her hubby's money. It was common knowledge around town that Spencer Lockhart doted on his beautiful wife. Surely he wouldn't mind sparing some loose change to help her get her business off the ground, now would he?

He cleared his oversize desk, which doubled as a worktable,

and dragged out a large sketch pad, began fiddling with ideas. This wasn't the sort of product that needed hype, just presentation. He didn't have to sell the idea of brides and weddings and fancy dresses; that had been done for him centuries ago. His mission was to present *these* dresses as *the* dresses to wear, what every fashionable bride should want. Too bad there wasn't a bride of marriageable age in the White House at the moment. Even Mike knew how much Priscilla of Boston had benefited after the Nixon girls' weddings—

"Mike?"

He looked up at Fran, standing in the doorway. "Yeah?"

"I tried Fairchild Bridals, but Miss Fairchild isn't in much, according to the manager. I asked if there was another number where we might reach her, but the woman only offered to take a message...."

"So try her at home," Mike said, refocusing on the drawing table.

"Earth to Mike? Her home number's not exactly listed in the phone book."

He glanced up. "Oh. You have a point." He collapsed back against his chair, tapping his pencil against the desk. "Did her manager sound as if she'd give her the message?"

Fran shrugged. "Who knows? She did sound like one of those protective types, though." She grinned. "Like me."

Mike winced. That could be bad news. Well, he supposed he could try to get through in person, use his charm and wit to weasel his way into this woman's heart and her boss's pocketbook.

He stood, slipping his jacket back on. "How old would you say this manager was?"

"What? Now you expect me to have X-ray vision, too? How should I know?"

With a patient breath, he said, "From her voice, Fran. What would you guess? Young, old, close to death, what?"

She shrugged. "Maybe under thirty. I don't know."

Hmm. He was generally more successful at charming older ladies than young. Well, except Fran. But then, Cary Grant probably couldn't have charmed Fran. In any case—he yanked his attention back to the matter at hand—younger women, he'd found, were usually too savvy to be easily ensnared.

No matter.

"What's the address?"

Fran handed him a pink While You Were Out slip. He glanced at it, nodded. Then looked at it again.

And remembered the sign on the front lawn of the old house he'd seen Friday night, when he'd gotten lost.

You don't suppose…?

"I'll be back in an hour, lovely lady," he said. "Oh—and go ahead and set up an appointment with Salvadore Rodriquez. Tell him I thought of a great publicity idea for his restaurant."

He was out the door before Fran had answered.

3

This was Monday. Since the salon was closed, Monday was supposed to be hers. But if Zoe didn't wade through the paperwork she'd put off on Friday, she'd be even more behind. And she supposed she should let Nancy, the assistant manager, take over more of the routine, day-to-day stuff. Still, the extra work kept her occupied. Kept her from thinking about... things.

Her bad mood had faded somewhat over the weekend. She'd done a wedding on Saturday, the last one for a month unless someone got sick, then spent all day Sunday cleaning her apartment. Not exactly thrills and chills, but the activity had tricked her into thinking she was accomplishing something worthwhile. So she'd gone to bed exhausted and somewhat at peace, and had slept through the night—a rare occurrence these last few months. Now, however, as she faced this mountain of paperwork, she wished she had a match.

Zoe barely heard the doorbell over the vintage Aretha blaring through the empty building. She had a real thing for the Motown sound, music from the decade before she was even born. But that was neither here nor there. What *was* here was the doorbell, which sounded as if it had gotten stuck.

Muttering, she tossed her pen on the desktop and stormed out to the door, yanking her turtleneck sweater down over her hips as she went. The rain had left a chill in its wake, and today felt decidedly like fall.

Through the pebbled glass panels she could make out *tall*

and probably *male*. It wasn't the UPS man, because he didn't come before four, and the mail had already come—

She stopped the stupid guessing game and opened the door. And her mouth.

Then she shut it. Her mouth, not the door. And glowered at him. He was smiling, the sort of smile that every intelligent female over the age of twelve learns *real* fast to avoid at all costs. And it didn't help things any that he wasn't sweating this time and that the very nice body she remembered much more clearly than she wanted to was very nicely clad in a very nice suit that cost enough to let her know that whatever he did, he was very good at it.

As if that mattered.

"You get lost again?" she asked.

His low, sexy chuckle was... Well, the shiver that shimmied up her spine had nothing to do with the cold air that had whisked into the foyer when she opened the door. She didn't like that. Well, she *did* like it, but that's what she didn't like. That she liked it.

Oh, hell.

"Well, this *is* a surprise!" He held out his hand. She noticed, illogically, that the ash trees in the front yard had begun to turn. In a week, less, all those thousands of tiny, fluttering leaves would be an almost iridescent yellow. Breathtaking against a blue sky...

"Mike Kwan, Miss...?"

She snapped her attention back to his face. "Why are you here?"

There went the smile again. And for the life of her, she couldn't look away. "Tell you what. Tell me your name, and I'll tell you why I'm here."

The words were pushy. Arrogant, even. But the voice... wasn't. He was teasing, to be sure. And Zoe didn't like to be teased. She didn't think, anyway. And he was as full of himself as they came.

But he wasn't mean. Why she knew that, she couldn't have

said. Neither did this revelation make her any less cautious. Still…

Still.

She pursed her lips. "Zoe Chan," she said with as little air expenditure as possible. She thought she saw his heavy brows twitch, for a second; a flicker of something in his eyes, but then wasn't sure.

"Miss Chan," he said, letting the smile blossom. "I own the Kwan Agency. I believe my assistant called earlier and spoke to someone about making an appointment with Miss Fairchild to discuss her advertising needs for her upcoming venture? Was that you she spoke with?"

She let him stew for several beats while she decided what, if anything, to say. Or do. Then she said, offhandedly, "Ohhh, right. I remember now. Mmm—we got several calls this morning. I guess because of the article."

No one ever said she was above lying.

"Several…calls," he echoed. Carefully, with a slight nod to his head.

"Yes." She smiled. "You're not the only advertising agency in town who sees the potential in Br—Miss Fairchild's expansion."

She crossed her arms and stared him down, wondering at what point over the weekend her anatomy had altered to include a certain male…apparatus. At least that made her equal with the guy in front of her, who, considering his gall at showing up uninvited and expecting to worm his way into an appointment, clearly had a blue-ribbon worthy set of his own.

Suddenly she had no idea where to focus. But she refused to blush.

"Maybe not," he allowed, and she knew he didn't believe her. "But I'll bet I'm the only one who already has a proposal worked up."

Oooh, this guy was smooth. But, then, so was milk of magnesia. Which, as she remembered all too clearly, left a disgusting aftertaste.

"Whether you do or not, since Miss Fairchild isn't here, it

doesn't matter. Now, if you'll excuse me, I was in the middle of—''

"When will she be in, then?''

"She doesn't keep a regular schedule. I have no idea.''

"Then let me discuss the proposal with you.''

Zoe blew out an impatient sigh. "*Mr.* Kwan—not only would that be a complete waste of both our times, but Miss Fairchild made her views on advertising explicitly clear in her interview—''

"And she couldn't have been more wrong," he interjected.

That did it. "Excuse me, but my employer has successfully run her business for five years. I assure you she knows exactly what she's doing, and what she does or does not need. Now I really must get back to work—''

She started to close the door, only to be flabbergasted when he actually put his foot in the way to stop it.

"And if she's as astute a businesswoman as you say she is, I doubt whether she'd be pleased to have missed a potential opportunity because her assistant's got a bug up her...because her assistant's in a mood.''

"And who the hell crowned you King of the Presumptuous?" she shot back. She pushed the door against his loafer, then glared at him. "It would be a lot easier to close the door without your foot in it, you know." She opened the door slightly. "Do you mind?''

A sudden puff of wind reached through the door and grabbed a fistful of her hair, whipping it into her face. She started to grab it, only to jump when her hand collided with Mike's as he got there first, gently removing the errant hank and smoothing it away from her face. His fingertips grazed her cheek for less than a second, still long enough for every nerve ending in her body to sound the alarm.

She stared at him, unable—or unwilling, she wasn't sure which—to move, aware of his fingers combing to the ends of her long hair with excruciating slowness. His eyes remained locked with hers, his brows hinting at a frown.

A succession of jolts rammed through her system, too rapid

to be reacted to one at a time. Her reaction to his gentle touch, to the slightly lost look in his eyes, to the realization of how long it had been since a man had touched her. Since she'd wanted one to.

And how much she suddenly ached for that touch.

"Your boss is very fortunate to have someone as loyal as you work for her," he said, every trace of arrogance gone from his voice. Or at least, so it seemed through the buzzing inside her head. Instead, she thought she heard a sort of wonder, maybe. Wistfulness.

Oy.

"If you would be so kind as to give her my message, I would really appreciate having the opportunity to discuss this with her." He reached inside his jacket, pulled out a business card, handed it to her. She took care that their fingers didn't touch. "And you, Miss Chan, as well. No obligation, I assure you. But I do think…" He hesitated, smiled. "I'd just like a chance to show her what I can do, that's all. Both of you might be surprised."

Surprises were obviously his forte, since she sure as hell wasn't expecting him to kiss her hand. Not just a cursory peck, either, but a lingering pressure of warm, soft lips on her knuckles. Then, with a slight bow that was almost old-fashioned, he left, skipping down the stairs and out to his Saturn.

Leaving Zoe to pick her teeth up off the porch floor.

There was a message from Brianna Fairchild Lockhart—he didn't miss the fact that she'd used all three names—waiting by the time he got back to the office. Fran handed it to him, her face a mask.

He poked his assistant in the arm with his wrist. "What did I tell you? Am I good or what?"

"You really don't want me to answer that, do you?"

"Probably not." He leafed through his other messages, waiting.

"So…what'd you do?" she finally asked, with just the slightest tinge of annoyance in her voice.

He slanted her a grin. "Thought you didn't want to know."

"You'll tell me anyway. Might as well get it over with."

"I kissed her assistant's hand."

"No!" Fran pretended to be horror-stricken. "Had to go that far down into the bag of tricks, did you?"

He remembered the pretty, indignant face he'd just left and thought he would've dug a helluva lot deeper to win *that* one over. And not just to get the Fairchild account, either. Suddenly, finding the chink in the feisty Miss Chan's armor had become a goal in its own right.

The feisty *Zoe* Chan...

"Mike? Yoo-hoo?" He was vaguely aware that Fran was waving in front of his face. Startled, he met her extremely curious eyes. "So...you wove one of your spells, huh?"

He looked down at the message. *Hold the phone.* Winning over Zoe Chan—or any other woman, for that matter—wasn't part of his game plan. Couldn't be. *Couldn't.*

"Yeah," he said on a sigh. "I guess I did. I guess...I better go make this call, then," he continued, dazed. "Yeah..."

"She said she'd be at that number until about three," Fran called out behind him as he drifted into his office.

"Okay...thanks."

The door snicked closed behind him; he leaned against it for a moment, scrubbing his hand over his face. Could it really be that he'd met, on his own and purely by chance—and *twice*, no less—the very woman he'd refused to have anything to do with? That he'd nearly severed his relationship with his grandfather over? It had to be...there were millions of Chans, but not that many Chinese Zoes.

She was bright, she was pretty, she was...

Not for him. Despite the glimmer of reciprocal interest he thought he saw in her eyes. Not the way his life was, with his nonstop schedule, his bizarre hours as the agency struggled to match Mike's growth projections for it in five years. Ten. There was no point going through this again, getting something started only to have to back out when it became clear—

again—that there really was no room in his life for a woman. Not the way he wanted a woman to be in his life, at any rate.

So, if they were to work together, he'd have to content himself with the verbal sparring matches. And the view. But no touching.

Definitely no touching.

His fingers found their way to his lips, still buzzing from the feel of her satiny smooth skin. His nostrils, too, tingled with her scent, a mixture of expensive hand lotion and… chrysanthemum petals, he realized. Oh, yeah…*this* one was danger personified. This one, if he wasn't careful, could undermine everything he'd been working toward for the last four years. And what he found especially unsettling was the realization that he might not even care.

Too late to back out now, he thought, picking up the phone and punching in Brianna Fairchild's number. Nobody had ever been able to call Mike Kwan a chicken. A damn fool, maybe, but not a chicken.

"Who in their right mind would pay a hundred twenty-five bucks for a crib bumper?" Zoe said, ignoring the saleslady's dagger looks from twenty feet away.

"Zoe! For the love of…" Margi caught herself, lowering her voice to a frantic hiss. "Obviously, people do," she said, rolling her eyes to indicate not only the fancy-schmanzy baby boutique, but the gaga-eyed parents-to-be shopping their frenzied little butts off.

Zoe harrumphed, then leaned toward her sister, whom she knew wouldn't spend that kind of money, either. "Just seems a waste, you know? Kid's just gonna either spit up or poop all over it. Might as well be on something cheap." She lifted up a Dior diaper cover. "Thirty bucks? I don't pay that for my *jeans*—Marg?" She looked around for her vanished sister. "Hey—where'd you go?"

Margi had already wheeled her cart to the checkout counter and was unloading her haul. "Remind me," she said through pursed lips when Zoe joined her, "the next time I decide to take you shopping with me to leave you at home."

Zoe grunted again, softly, then leaned against the counter, deliberately grinning at the unamused saleswoman, who seemed as anxious as Margi to complete the transaction and get Zoe out of her store. She knew she was being insufferable, but she couldn't seem to stop herself. "I'm the bargain hunter in the family," she said with unabashed pride. "I've never paid full price for anything in my life."

"Zo—*cut it out!*" Margi growled under her breath as the saleswoman allowed, "How nice for you" between clenched teeth.

Deciding she'd tortured everyone enough for the moment, Zoe did as her sister requested. Once they were out of the shop, Margi said on a sigh, "So, did I do something special to deserve being humiliated like that, or is this just the mood you're in today?"

Zoe had been in a mood, all right, ever since Mike Kwan's appearance at the salon two days ago. He'd rattled her cage so hard her teeth hurt. But she wasn't about to let her sister in on *that* little episode. Especially as she hadn't yet figured it out herself. So she shrugged and steered the cumbersome woman in the direction of the cookie kiosk in the center of the mall. "A little of both, I suppose. You want chocolate-chip pecan or double chocolate chunk? My treat."

"And now you're going to ply me with cookies?"

"Yep," Zoe said, struggling to get her wallet out of her tote bag. "So which is it?"

"Double chocolate chunk. Ouch!"

Zoe threw Margi a concerned glance. "Hey, honey—you okay?"

"Oh, yeah. It's just these damn Braxton-Hicks contractions. Every time Junior here rams his foot in a certain spot, it sets them off." Zoe paid for the cookies, then led Margi over to a bench and commanded her to sit.

"I'm supposed to walk."

"You have been walking, airhead. For two hours. Look, I

don't know about you, but the idea of your birthing this kid in the middle of Phipps Plaza does not appeal, okay? So sit.''

"Don't be ridiculous, Zo. I'm not due until the end of October. I told you—'' she grunted like a walrus plopping on an ice floe as she lowered herself to the bench ''—these aren't real contractions.''

They settled their bags around them as Zoe fished out a cookie and handed it to her sister. "You also told me that first-time mothers aren't supposed to have these contractions this much.''

"Sheesh, Zo, lighten up, would you? I just saw the doctor today. I'm fine. Junior's fine. We're all fine.'' Swallowing the bite in her mouth, she nailed her with her best Older Sister look. "Or are we?''

"What are you talking about?'' Zoe asked, knowing damn well what Margi was talking about.

"You. After that stunt you pulled on Friday night, not coming to dinner—''

"Mom and I got that all worked out, Marg. Butt out.''

"I can't. Butting out's genetically impossible for a Chan.''

"You're not a Chan anymore, remember? You've left your father's house for your husband's—''

"Nice try, Zo. What is going on with you?''

If she didn't tell her sister something, anything, the woman would never leave her alone. So she took another bite of cookie, a large enough one to preclude conversation for the next few minutes, and thought.

And decided to make the most of the opportunity.

"You wanna know what's been bugging me?'' she said at last. "What really set me off?'' She swiveled on the bench and met her sister's questioning gaze. "That you and Van and Ma won't leave me alone about my love life. Or whatever one could call my currently manless state. I had forgotten that Friday was the one-year anniversary of Walter's little revelation. Forgotten, I suppose, because for the last year that's exactly what I've been trying to do. Forget. Well, that didn't work. I don't need to put Walter's betrayal out of my thoughts, but remember it. Vividly and in excruciating detail. Because by remembering, I'll stay safe.''

Her sister tried to interrupt, but Zoe wouldn't let her.

"I'm tired of dating, Marg. It's a colossal waste of time and energy, far as I can tell. So I'm not doing it anymore. Not for you or Ma or anyone else.''

She stopped to take a breath, which was just long enough for Margi to jump in with both barrels blazing.

"And if you don't date, how do you expect to meet anybody? Or do you plan to spend the rest of your life in your apartment, watching TV and eating microwave dinners? When you're not up to your eyeballs in other peoples' weddings, that is?''

"I don't *plan* on doing anything one way or the other,'' Zoe said. "But I certainly have no desire to spend one more evening of my life with one more loser, okay?''

To her annoyance, Mike Kwan's earnest expression popped into her thought, the feel of his fingers on her cheek, his warm breath on the back of her hand. She might still find him presumptuous and pushy, but he was not, by any stretch of her overworked imagination, a loser.

Margi had been unusually silent, Zoe realized. Which was not a good sign. Then she said, "Just do us one favor.''

Zoe's antennae sprang to attention. "No.''

"Just go out one more time—''

"Forget it, Marg—''

"—with Mr. Wu's grandson—''

"No!''

"I'm *sure* this guy's different,'' Margi was saying, but Zoe had covered her ears and was shaking her head from side to side. When her sister reached up and yanked down her hands, Zoe preempted her strike.

"Listen to me, Marg. And you can tell Vanessa and Ma, too. If you guys don't get off my back about this, I swear I'll stay as far away from all of you as I can.''

"Oh, don't be melodramatic, Zoe.''

"I'm not. I'm dead serious.''

Something in Margi's expression shifted. The concern was still there, plain as ever, but tempered now, Zoe thought, with a little surprise.

"This is really important to you, isn't it?"

"Oh, hallelujah! The light dawns!" With a tremendous sigh, she took her sister's hands in hers. "I really, really need the space to do whatever it is I'm supposed to be doing. I have no idea what that's supposed to be, granted, but I can hardly *breathe* when I'm around you guys. And I hate that. I love you both—and Ma—to distraction, and I understand that you just want me to be happy. And I've always wanted to make you happy, to do whatever you asked because I trusted you had my best interests at heart. That's great and wonderful and all that, but I'm twenty-six. I don't need to be shepherded, ya know?"

After a moment, Margi nodded. Her mouth was set, and her brows were pulled down into a borderline scowl, but she gave in.

"So…you promise to back off?" Zoe asked.

"Yeah," her sister let out on an exasperated breath.

"And tell the others?"

"Yeah, yeah…*okay!*" Then Margi rubbed her stomach and pushed herself off the bench. "You wanna come back with me to the apartment for dinner?"

Zoe laughed. "We had dinner before we went shopping, remember?"

Margi looked perplexed for a moment. "Did we? Oh…I guess we did, huh? Well, tough noogies. I'm hungry." She brushed a layer of cookie crumbs off the front of her maternity jumper and began ambling down the concourse. "You think the Golden Dragon is still open? Maybe I could get a pint of cashew chicken to go."

Zoe offered to go into the restaurant to get Margi's takeout while Margi stayed in the car. Much as her normally energetic sister was loath to admit it, the pregnancy was beginning to take its toll.

It was nearly closing time; the seating area was virtually empty, several of the kitchen staff having their dinner at a large round table near the back.

Zoe smiled at the lone cashier, a chipmunk of a man with a quick grin and a buzz cut that looked like a neglected lawn. "I've got a starving preggo out in the car who would kill for a pint of cashew chicken," she said, leaning heavily on the counter. "What are the chances of getting some?"

"Oh, man…" The guy chuckled, sweeping one hand over the black thatch on his head. "Pregnant women are the worst, aren't they? I've considered hooking up my wife to an IV. If she gets me up one more time at three in the morning, I just may—hey, Mike!"

"Evening, Randy. Hot sour soup, beef and broccoli… Miss Chan?"

Startled, Zoe whipped around and looked up—way up—into Mike Kwan's smiling face, more than a little flummoxed at the curious lurch in her chest. His hair was a bit unkempt, skirting the collar of his taupe trench coat, but his tie still held its perfect Windsor knot. She glanced at the briefcase in his hand and guessed that, at 9:00 p.m., he had come to the restaurant straight from work. Her gaze drifted back to those up-to-no-good eyes, and caught the weariness there. And something else. The pang of empathy that shot through her stole her breath.

She looked away so quickly, her neck popped.

"That'll be about ten minutes, folks," the cashier said, then swept into the back.

"We might as well sit down while we wait," Mike said, gesturing toward the bench across from the cash register.

Zoe suddenly found her velour sweat suit far too warm.

"No…thanks," she said, hitching the straps of her purse up onto her shoulder. "I'd rather stand."

Electric smile and twinkling eyes notwithstanding, she didn't trust this guy. Didn't want to. Trust led to broken promises, and broken hearts. And thank you very much, she didn't need either in her life again. *Nice guys* were not part of her karma.

Mike regarded her for a moment, his expression serious. Then, with a sharp nod, he sat down.

She stood with her back to him, trying to convince herself it didn't matter one whit whether he was watching her or not. She prayed, as fervently as she'd ever prayed for anything, that Margi the Matchmaker stayed in the car. One look at this guy and her sister would have the wedding invitations in the mail.

Mike prayed that his grandfather had already left for the night. If the old man caught wind that Mike had already met Zoe, he'd have the wedding banquet arranged within minutes. A thought which Mike didn't find entirely unattractive.

He doubted, however, that Zoe felt the same way. Two days ago he thought he'd detected a spark of attraction on her part, even if an unwilling one. Tonight he decided it must have been the light. She clearly wasn't interested, though whether her disaffection was directed toward him or toward relationships in general, he couldn't say. Unfortunately, each time he saw her, everything he'd told himself—and his grandfather—about why he couldn't commit to anyone seemed to lose ground.

But still.

He was navigating a minefield, and he knew it. And he knew why. A born salesman, he couldn't resist the challenge to turn every "no" into a "yes." Resistance was something to be conquered, not submitted to. But he'd always proceeded from the understanding that whatever he was trying to sell—whether himself or a campaign—was in everyone's best interest.

He doubted that was the case this time. After all, he had no idea what or who this woman was, what sort of baggage she lugged around with her. But he did know what sort of baggage he lugged around with *him.* And that alone should be enough to keep him from making a serious mistake. Even though he'd always been up-front about his work habits and his dedication to his business, every woman he'd dated more than twice had thought she could change him, convince him to put his career second.

There'd been more than a few disappointed women over the past few years. Not exactly something he was proud of.

He lay his head back against the bench cushion and shut his eyes, listening to the small, slim woman in front of him chat with the cashier. On the surface, she sounded perfectly at ease. But Mike had spent far too long learning how to read what was below the surface to buy into her studied nonchalance. Whether it was his presence, or something else entirely, that had put her on guard, he didn't know. But she *was* on guard. Of that much he was sure. A certain tightness in her voice, a hint of unnaturalness about her laugh—the signs were so blatant, to anyone who knew what to look for, that it was almost comical. Judging from their previous encounters, though, he didn't figure Zoe Chan as the cautious type. Unless...

He opened his eyes in time to see her eyes dart away. Unless...she'd been hurt. And if that was the case, then it was even more imperative that he keep his distance. After all, he was no longer a kid. And neither was she. He was too old, and too tired, to play anymore.

Unless, he thought as an unfamiliar ache coiled in the center of his chest, it was for keeps.

Not a moment too soon, one of the kitchen boys brought out their food. Zoe peered into her bag, saw two containers instead of one, and sighed. She held out the bag to Mike. Realized she could almost feel her mother's swat on her rump as she commanded, "*Smile,* for goodness' sake!"

She smiled. "He mixed up our orders."

After a cursory glance inside his own bag, Mike made the switch without further comment. But then, instead of leaving, they simply stood in front of each other like two kids forced to dance with each other at a party.

Mike cleared his throat. "I suppose you know I'm coming to the salon tomorrow to give a presentation?"

"Yes. Yes, of course I know that," she said, perhaps more sharply than she meant. But he was making her nervous. More nervous. She needed to leave, preferably before she did something stupid. For the past ten minutes she'd been more aware of him than she'd ever been of a man in her life. The pull toward…whatever it was that pulled humans to each other, was suffocatingly strong. Hypnotic. She'd only felt half this attracted to Walter, and look what that had gotten her.

This was nuts. What was she, a bee attracted to a lousy flower?

"My sister's waiting," she said, holding up the package.

"Oh, of course. Well…see you tomorrow," he said, then turned toward the door.

"Hey, wait a minute…." She grabbed his sleeve, let go the instant he looked at her. "Didn't you forget to pay?"

Something resembling embarrassment crossed his face before his mouth hitched into a lopsided smile. "I eat here or take out nearly every night," he said, nodding at the cashier. "I, uh, have an account."

She wouldn't have thought the imperious Mr. Wu would have allowed accounts, but who was she to argue the point? As the cashier had remained silent, she supposed there was nothing else to say.

"Oh, I see. Well, that's all right, then."

He wagged his head, chuckling.

"What?"

"Nothing, nothing." He lifted the bag again, in a kind of salute. "'Night, Miss Chan. See you tomorrow."

Despite the fact that this was none of her business, the minute Mike was gone, Zoe asked the cashier, "He really has an account?"

The guy gave a half laugh. "You might say that, since he's—"

One side of the double wooden doors swung open,

whooshed closed with a soft thud. "Sheesh, lady—they tie you up in here?"

Zoe turned at the sound of her sister's voice, the cashier forgotten. "It's okay. I've got it, see?"

Margi winced, rubbing her belly even as she lustfully eyed the bag.

"Come on, Miss Preggo," Zoe said. "I'll drive. You can eat in the car."

Her sister grabbed the bag, opened it, rummaged for the plastic fork in the bottom. "Car, hell. I'll starve by then."

Zoe guided her sister out the door as the woman attacked the cashew chicken as if she hadn't eaten in three days. Thank God Margi was too preoccupied to talk. Or even look at her.

The prospect of seeing Mike again, Zoe realized, was not sitting well. The weird thing was, though, when she thought about the next day, she couldn't decide if the churning in her stomach was due to dread...or anticipation.

The one thing Mike hadn't counted on, he mused as he tried to sweet talk Brianna Fairchild Lockhart, was that sweet talk bounced off the businesswoman's cool veneer like water beaded up on oilcloth. Not that he was surprised, actually. But if he was about to make an idiot of himself, he would rather not have done it in front of Zoe Chan. Whither went the violin, however, so went the bow.

The conference had already gone on for about twenty minutes. Miss Fairchild leaned back in her chair, squinting at Mike and thoughtfully sucking on the end of a pen. She was one of the most composed women he'd ever met, her elegant beauty enhanced by her upswept honey-blond hair, her expensive pearl gray wool suit, the simple strand of pearls and matching earrings. By contrast, her quivering assistant, seated immediately on her right, seemed incapable of stillness for any discernible duration. Her long, loose hair slithered over her shoulders and grazed the tabletop as she took what seemed to be copious notes on the meeting, while multicolored stones from her heavily embroidered and beaded black vest glinted restlessly in the late-afternoon sunlight streaming through the windows behind her. If Miss Fairchild was Saks, her assistant was Pier One. Yet Brianna clearly took Zoe's opinion very seriously.

An opinion he wished he could read. Zoe had hardly even looked at him since the meeting had begun. Although he did think—hope—he saw a trace of appreciation flicker across her otherwise expressionless features at some of the options he'd mentioned.

"You think of me as a cash cow, don't you, Mr. Kwan?" Miss Fairchild now asked in her breathy voice.

Though Mike had to snap himself out of his reverie, he never missed a beat. "I'm not unaware of your resources, Miss Fairchild" was his candid reply. Perhaps he wasn't above manipulation, in the right circumstances, but coyness—his own or anyone else's—had always set his teeth on edge.

"Nor of my husband's, I'm sure."

They eyed each other for a moment. Mike had played easier chess games. Unfortunately, by not answering fast enough, he inadvertently blinked.

"I thought so," she said, as he noticed Zoe's eyes narrow at him from across the table.

"Miss Fairchild, let me explain—"

"Mr. Kwan," she said, leaning forward on the table, her hands clasped in front of her, "I run my company entirely on whatever resources I have on hand and what the bank will lend me. I refuse to touch a penny of my husband's money for my venture. Now, while I have no reservations about the ingenuity and quality of your campaign, this is a bridal gown company. I'm not selling jeans or sportswear or automobiles. All I have to do is get enough buyers to stock my gowns, and the brides will come. Most women try on at least twenty gowns before making a decision. Odds are that at least a couple of mine will be among those they try on. Barring a major fluke, the sales will happen without my spending a fortune on advertising."

Now Mike leaned forward, assuming a mirror image to

Brianna's. His hunch was that, while she knew more than most about marketing, preconceived notions were blinding her to possibilities. Or so he hoped. "Okay..." He rubbed one finger across his lips, then folded his hands back together. "Tell me something. When a bride comes in here to get her wedding gown, how often does she mention brand names?"

Brianna leaned back again in her chair, slightly twisted to one side. A masculine posture, he noted. "About half the time," she admitted.

"And how do they know these brand names?"

He caught the glance Brianna flicked in Zoe's direction, as well as the slightest tremor at the corner of her mouth. "Various sources. Relatives, friends..." She paused, her eyes dancing with mischief.

"And the others?" he prompted, knowing she was deliberately sidestepping the real answer.

At this, Brianna smiled. "Touché, Mr. Kwan," she said in her soft Southern accent. "Okay, you win. Yes...they've seen ads in magazines. And before you ask, yes again—most of the brides who've come in with the intent to buy a particular vendor's product will buy that product. But..." She held up one finger. "I don't necessarily need an agency to place an ad in a bridal magazine."

"But you probably would to put one in *Vogue*."

She laughed, a little breathlessly. "*Vogue* doesn't run bridal gown ads, Mr. Kwan."

"Not before this, that's true."

"Brianna," Zoe interjected, her neat black brows crumpled in a frown. "I know that would be very expensive—"

But Miss Fairchild held up one hand, gently cutting her off. "Hang on a minute, Zo. I agree—I can't exactly see how that would be cost-effective, but let's hear the man out."

This was his chance, then. Probably his only one.

"Miss Fairchild..." He hesitated, choosing his words. "Whether you use your husband's money or not is your decision. And a commendable one at that. But you can't hide from the fact that you're not exactly Sally Smith anymore.

You are Brianna Lockhart, as far as the world sees it, and as such, what's the harm in using your husband's name to further your career—?''

"Because, Mr. Kwan, if I can't make this venture a success on my own merits, then I'd rather chuck it and try something else, that's why. In case you missed it,'' she said softly, "women don't need to rely on a man to get ahead anymore.''

He looked to Zoe, whose eyes were flashing like the stones on her vest. "And that's not at all what I'm suggesting,'' Mike parried, realizing he was sinking fast. "It's not your husband's name I'm suggesting you take advantage of as much as the position his name gives you—''

Oh, brother.

Both women simply stared at him. Watching him hang himself, no doubt.

"Look,'' he said quickly. But calmly, he hoped. "Trying to sell *anything* these days is a cut-throat business. Without some sort of advantage, a business will go belly-up faster than a dead fish. While your product is beautiful, there's nothing to separate it in your customers' eyes from any of the other bridal manufacturers out there, all of whom have the advantage of reputation on their sides.''

"So I'll advertise in the bridal magazines. On my own. I don't see what—''

"But advertising in a *fashion* magazine would give an edge over your competitors. And only your name will get a fashion magazine to accept your ad. Brianna Lockhart going into a national—maybe even international—market is newsworthy, don't you see? All I'm suggesting is…''

But Miss Fairchild had stood. Although she was smiling, Mike recognized the set to her mouth. He'd seen it far too often on his mother's, when he'd asked one too many times for something she didn't think he should have.

"Mr. Kwan—I appreciate your time and interest, but I'm afraid you're barking up the wrong tree.'' She held out her hand. "I have your card. Should I need your services at some point down the road, I'll be sure to call.'' After a brief handshake, she said to Zoe, "Would you mind showing Mr. Kwan out? I didn't realize how late it was—I need to pick up Melissa at playgroup by four."

As he watched the tall woman leave the room, he wondered, for a second, if he was losing his touch.

It had been a long time since Zoe had disagreed with Brianna. But she sure as shootin' disagreed with her now.

She'd been so sure Mike was full of hot air, just another huckster out to make a buck, with his charming smile and carefully modulated voice and the expensive after-shave and the way his navy blazer hugged his broad shoulders....

Zoe shook her head quickly, as if trying to jerk herself awake. As they made their way down the hall, Mike shifted in her direction, his brows raised in question.

"You okay?"

She lifted her face to his, instantly looked somewhere else. "Oh, yeah, fine. I'm just thinking..."

She let her voice trail off, trying not to let his scent muddle her thoughts any more than it already had. He wasn't supposed to be good. His ideas weren't supposed to be solid. Shoot— they were downright brilliant, some of them, and perfectly suited to Brianna's goals for the company.

Zoe hadn't expected substance beneath the charm. No, she admitted, with a sharp little sigh. She hadn't *wanted* there to be substance beneath the charm.

But there was.

The man might be arrogant and a mite too self-confident, but he was clearly no slouch. Even if his delivery had come across a touch on the chauvinistic side—so the guy wasn't perfect—he had a point. Why *shouldn't* Brianna take advantage of her position and name to promote the line? If her stuff was mediocre, that would be one thing. But it wasn't. The designs were gorgeous and meticulously crafted. What could a little boost hurt? The ad in *Vogue* would be just the ticket. And Zoe knew Brianna could afford it, despite her protests, even without Spencer's money. Besides, many of his other ideas for promotion would be virtually free—talk shows, charity luncheons, a syndicated interview to go into Sunday papers across the country.

Fairchild Bridals needed Mike Kwan's expertise. And time. With all their other duties, neither Zoe nor Brianna could manage a campaign on this scale. Surely Brianna would understand that.

But Zoe didn't need, or want, Mike Kwan anywhere near her. She could pretend all she wanted, but the fact remained that she was far too attracted to him, aware of him, for her own good. She was neither in the mood for an unrequited crush, nor for a relationship that would only end as all her others had ended—in the toilet.

"Well," he said, interrupting her thoughts. "Guess you proved me wrong."

She was suddenly aware that she had stepped closer to him than necessary; she nonchalantly drifted away. "I tried to warn you," she said, unable to resist rubbing it in.

"Yeah." His sideways glance made her face tingle, though she had no idea why. "You did."

"But you were too stubborn to listen."

He grunted a short laugh. "I believe the politically correct term is *persistent*."

"Mm. People have said the same thing about me, too," she admitted. "Although they're usually walking around in ever-narrowing circles—" she made a circular motion in the air with her fingertip "—and muttering incoherently at the time."

He laughed at that, and Zoe mentally smacked herself. Why the hell was she flirting with him? And that's what it was, wasn't it? Good Lord…just like some mush-brained adolescent. Unfortunately, joking to make people feel better was a reflex. Funny, though—she rarely considered what it might be like to have someone do that for *her*. As she did with anything else she couldn't control, she simply didn't think about it too much. When she was around Mike, however, the sequestered thought crept out of its hidey-hole and blew raspberries at her, reminding her that, like it or not, her life had a few chinks in it. And some of them were whoppers.

Having Mike in her life, however peripherally, would remind her of what she didn't have. Not a pleasant prospect. But—she hauled in a breath—she couldn't let her personal feelings influence what was right for the business.

For Brianna, she told herself, she'd make this sacrifice.

They'd reached the waiting room; Nancy brought her some papers to check over. After a minute's conversation, the girl returned to the reception desk. Zoe turned back to Mike, who was admiring the room.

"Beautiful," he said simply. Appreciatively. Oblivious to the half-dozen dumbstruck women sitting in the middle of the room he was so casually surveying, he stuck one hand in his pants pocket, striking the quintessential male catalog-model pose. Unbidden, Zoe's thoughts wandered to his appearance when she'd first seen him, half-naked and glistening with sweat, his hair—now so neatly framing those luscious cheekbones, that high, broad brow—mussed and dripping wet and sticking to his forehead over his sweatband. At the time, she remembered feeling a tremor of what she'd thought was distaste.

She'd been wrong. So very, very wrong.

"I love the way all the different styles work together. That highboy over there—" he nodded toward the far side of the room "—is it Hepplewhite?"

"I'm...not really sure," she hedged, annoyed he'd gained the upper hand. She had an eye for quality, she supposed, but had never paid much attention to periods or styles. "I'm no antiques expert. But I know it's old. It was one of the few things Brianna took from her parents' house after her father died, several years ago." Curiosity got the better of her. "How do you know so much about collectibles?"

"Blame my mother. She used to drag me and my father all over the countryside to estate sales when I was a kid." He grinned. "I learned more than I thought I would, considering all I cared about was the football or baseball or soccer game I was probably missing. It all worked out, though.''

''Oh?''

His shoulders lifted in a quick shrug. ''Yeah. I don't have much time for sports anymore, but I've got some great pieces of furniture and art in my apartment that I can enjoy any time I'm home.'' The smile faded around the edges. ''Not that I am, all that much, but…'' He shook his head as if to clear it. ''Well.'' He started to edge his way to the door. ''Since I've just been rejected, I guess that's that—''

''Mike, wait.'' She closed the gap between them, laying a hand on his sleeve. Through layers of wool and broadcloth, her sensitive fingers felt the muscles in his forearm flex, sending a jolt of awareness zinging up her arm. Flustered, she jerked her hand back. ''Actually…''

His eyes were pinned to hers. Amused eyes, she thought. Cocky, maybe. Curious, definitely. And, again, everything in her said to let it go. Brianna would do fine without Mike Kwan. Though probably not nearly as well as *Zoe* would do without Mike Kwan. Then, from her own mouth of all places, she heard, ''Actually, I have an idea. Come here.'' She did an about-face, beckoning him to follow.

A half-dozen pairs of female eyes followed, as well.

She led him past the alteration and millinery workroom in the back of the salon, into a small storage room in which the new samples for Market had been carefully hung in oversize clear plastic garment bags.

''How badly do you want this account?'' Zoe asked.

He was already pawing through the covered dresses. ''I'm here, aren't I?''

Zoe nodded, then stepped up beside him and flipped through the gowns, tugging one off the rack and carrying it into one of the smaller dressing rooms, Mike following like an obedient pup. She hauled the heavy gown from its plastic shroud and spread it out in front of him, trying hard not to gasp herself.

Even without a body to fill it out, it was spectacular in its simplicity—tissue taffeta the color of rich cream, tucked diagonally across the fitted, dropped waist bodice, then exploding into a billowing skirt. But what made the gown the stuff of fairy tales and fantasy were the hundreds of quivering handmade silk roses, edged in glittering organza leaves, that completely edged the off-the-shoulder neckline, drifting in a diagonal line across the bodice to curve in a majestic sweep across the front of the skirt.

"Wow," Mike said, and she couldn't help a chuckle. He knelt down in front of it, skimming the glistening fabric with his fingertips. "This is...incredible. How much does something like this go for?"

Zoe told him, which got a whistle of appreciation. "Hell," he said, rising again to his feet. "I think I'm in the wrong business."

"Brianna's brilliant," she said carefully, "but she doesn't always know what's best for her. It takes a lot of nagging and convincing, sometimes, before she finally sees the light." She paused. "And you didn't exactly rack up the Brownie points with your approach."

His eyes lit up. "So *that's* why you kept glaring at me like that. Trying to get me to shut up."

"*Now* you catch on," she said with a laugh, catching her reflection in the three way mirror on the other side of the room as she held the dress to her breasts, the shimmering taffeta like whipped cream under her fingertips. In four years, she'd seen thousands of wedding dresses. This was the first time, however, she'd felt the urge to try one on.

She suddenly remembered she wasn't alone. When she looked back at Mike, she was met with another one of his puzzled expressions. And the breath of a smile playing around a mouth too beautifully shaped for *anyone's* good. "Zoe...what are you saying?"

Oh, Lord. She really was losing it, wasn't she? Here she was, trying to conduct business, and what was she doing instead? Playing pretend.

Something she hadn't done since she was eight. This was hardly the time—or the place—for a revival of the practice.

"Can you do a mock-up of the *Vogue* ad," she said in a level voice, "to show Brianna exactly what you had in mind? I mean, you'd have to do it out of your pocket, and you might not want to do that...."

She watched his face, the way his mouth twitched for a second before spreading into a broad smile. "Anybody ever tell you how devious you are?"

The blush caught her by surprise. "Frequently."

"And...you're putting your neck in the noose by suggesting this, aren't you?"

"Absolutely." She crushed the dress to her, momentarily regretting her impulsiveness. "You won't tell?"

"Are you kidding? I live for this sort of thing." He came closer, reaching out. She flinched, thinking he was going to touch her. He hesitated, his eyes lightly brushing hers for a moment, before his fingers came to light on one of the roses. "I've got a photographer friend who owes me one," he said softly, and part of her wished she was that rose.

He was *way* too close. Almost abruptly, she whisked the gown away and crossed back to where its cover lay like a discarded skin on the damask settee.

"And can...can you do this like...tonight?"

"Tonight—?"

"I'll pick up the gown from your agency early tomorrow morning." The best thing was to just barge ahead as if it was a done deal, and everything would fall into place. "If Brianna gets wind that this is out of the salon, I'm dead." Which she didn't think was exactly true, but she didn't want to find out. She stuffed the enormous gown back into its bag, zipping it up. "Just, whatever you do, for *God's* sake, don't get it dirty," she admonished, picking up the bag and practically shoving it into his arms.

She could see a thousand questions in those dark, unreadable eyes. "Why are you doing this?" he asked.

Zoe knew what he was asking. She wished he hadn't. Shifting from one foot to the other in front of him, she said, "Because...because I think you're right and Brianna isn't."

They stood there, staring at each other.

"So-o-o," he said, dragging out the word as he shifted the heavy, unwieldy bag to his other arm. "This is strictly... *business?*" His gaze was so unnervingly direct it would have taken her breath away if she'd been able to breathe.

Flipping a hank of hair behind her ear, she said, "Sure. What else?"

"I just wondered...." He shrugged his shoulders.

She felt her eyes grow wide, her face warm. "You mean..." She nearly choked on the words. "You mean you thought I was *flirting* with you—?"

His brows collapsed into a frown. "Well, no, not exactly—"

"Oh, come on—what on earth did I do for you to think that?" What *had* she done? Had it been that obvious? And besides, what gentleman would mention such a thing? Where did he get off, assuming she was about to put her job at risk, for heaven's sake, for him?

"I'm sorry. I obviously misinterpreted—"

"My, my...aren't we impressed with ourselves?" she said, cutting him off. Then she walked briskly from the dressing room, assuming he'd get the message. "Hate to disappoint you, buster," she tossed over her shoulder in a fierce whisper, "but I rarely find chauvinistic presumption very attractive. In fact, I find it pretty obnoxious. And in my book, *obnoxious* and *attractive* are mutually exclusive terms."

Silence vibrated between them as they crossed through the reception area and out onto the covered porch. Then they both came to a halt, Zoe standing with her arms tightly crossed over her ribs, Mike clutching the white bagged gown in his arms as if he were strangling The Pillsbury Doughboy.

"Obnoxious?" he finally puffed out in a cloud of frosted air.

The damp cold instantly penetrated the loosely knit sweater she was wearing underneath her vest. "Y-yes," she said, shakily, too stubborn to take back her words. Besides, she'd meant it. More or less.

"I see." He seemed to consider this as he descended the porch steps and strode out to his car. Shivering now, she watched him open the back door, carefully spread out the bagged gown over the seat, then straighten up. "You know," he called to her over the Saturn's roof, "I'm beginning to understand why people end up nuts around you." His voice was much colder than the temperature. And *this* chill, she realized, knifed right to her heart. "Maybe I misjudged what was going on, but it was an offhand comment. All you needed to say was that I'd been mistaken. Perhaps—" he looked away for a moment, then back at her, and she saw a hurt in his eyes that stole her breath "—perhaps you should pay closer attention to how your employer deals with people, even when she doesn't agree with them. Now *there's* a lady."

He ducked into his car and was gone.

Once again, Zoe was left standing on the porch, watching Mike drive away. Once again, he'd managed to totally throw her for a loop. The last time, however, she hadn't felt like slime.

4

Now Zoe would barely talk to him.

Knee-jerk reactions were obviously her forte, he thought with a sigh as he poured himself a cup of coffee in the outer office, ignoring the phone ringing away on Fran's desk. But they were both grown-ups, for God's sake. Barbs like that should just bounce off.

Oh, yeah—they'd both really acted like grown-ups, hadn't they?

Of course, had her comment not hit its mark, he wouldn't have made the comeback he had....

Ellen, his copywriter, stuck her head out the door to her office. "We still on for ten o'clock about the Silverstone campaign? Wade wants to know." She grinned. "As usual, he's behind but is too chicken to tell you himself—"

"Am not!" came the indignant rebuttal from inside the office. "I just need to know if there've been any changes, that's all—"

Mike lifted his coffee mug toward the copywriter. "Tell Wade I'll give him fifteen minutes extra. And for that, he better damn sight give me brilliant."

The instant Ellen disappeared, Zoe reappeared in his thought.

She'd come for the dress at eight that morning, hardly commenting on the photograph proof—which was, even he had to admit, remarkable. He saw, or thought he did anyway, a spark of approval in her eyes. But her mouth remained drawn, her jaw tight. He found it next to impossible not to be irritated with her lack of enthusiasm. Getting the shoot done that fast was no mean feat. It had cost Mike a pretty penny and a couple of prime Falcons tickets. And had the model not been the photographer's live-in girlfriend, he still probably wouldn't have been able to pull it off.

Still, he'd played it cool.

"I'll get an eleven-by-fourteen made up today," he'd said, "and bring it over whenever you say."

"Fine," had been her lukewarm reply. "Brianna will be in all afternoon, as far as I know. If I hear differently, I'll give you a call."

If he'd had half a brain, he'd have apologized. But stubbornness wouldn't let him. He *didn't* like the way she judged people—him, anyway. And besides, how could she construe one lousy comment into *obnoxious?* Okay, so maybe it hadn't been the brightest comment in the world, but come on. He was obviously having an off day. A *very* off day. So he'd let her walk out. And had been cursing himself ever since.

While he was reliving this pitiful little scene, Fran arrived, slightly breathless from the brisk walk she forced herself to take every morning. Not that it seemed to do any good—the woman seemed destined to be "thick-waisted", as she called it, for the rest of her life. But then, she pointed out, think how heavy she'd be if she *didn't* walk.

"Whew!" she exhaled, plopping down in her chair to remove her walking shoes and put on her heels. "I swear someone added a couple of blocks last night when I was asleep." She bent over to slip on her shoes, peering at him over the edge of her desk. "What's with you?"

Mike frowned. "Do you think I'm obnoxious?"

"Oh, Lord," came the disembodied voice from the other side of the desk. Bobbing back into view, she asked, "Is this a surmisal or have you actually been accused?"

"The latter."

"Knew it would happen one day," Fran said on a sigh, fluffing her hair out from her neck.

"What's that supposed to mean?"

"It means that, yes, you get a little…pushy at times. Not to mention know-it-all, overbearing, imperious…" She lifted her face to him. "And you do tend to blurt out things without thinking them through—"

"Okay, okay, I get the picture." He studied her for a minute. "Do you hate me, too?"

She tossed him a squint on her way to the coffeemaker. "I hear two distinct questions in there, Michael. First, do I hate you?" She paused, filled her mug with coffee, stirred in one packet of Equal, one level tablespoon of Cremora. Took a sip. Finally continued her thought. "Right. I'm a total masochist, chaining myself to this nutso job every day because I think you're a jerk. No, doofus, I don't hate you. Besides being all those other things, you're generous and kind and appreciative and bright—well, most of the time, anyway—and basically a great boss. And if you get a swelled head from my saying that, I take it all back. Second…" She took another sip, her hips settled against the front of her desk. "Who is the 'too,' as in, do I hate you, *too?*"

To his immense chagrin, he felt himself blush. "Just a figure of speech, Fran."

"And is this 'figure of speech' the one who accused you of being obnoxious?"

He glared at his assistant. "Next time, remind me to hire someone dumb."

"Now, there's a left-handed compliment if ever I heard one." She shook her head as she walked around her desk, removed the plastic cover from her computer. "She cute?"

"Cute? Criminy, Fran…we back in junior high?"

She chuckled, unperturbed. "Is she?"

"Adorable," he growled, then stormed into his office and slammed the door.

Much to Zoe's relief, Brianna's annoyance with her little trick immediately vanished when she saw the ad mock-up. An exquisite brunette, standing in a pool of light that faded to blackness around the edges, modeled the gown against a starkly simple background. The "bride" held a single crystal candlestick in her hand, her other hand shielding the flame. The chiaroscuro effect delineated each rose petal, each fold and tuck of the gown, to perfection. This was no typical bridal ad. And Brianna admitted that Mike had caught exactly the sort of "feel" she wanted for her line, and the brides who would wear her dresses.

They were in the office. Mike had been gone twenty minutes or so. Down the hall, Zoe heard Betty shepherding a flock of tittering bridesmaids into the largest dressing room, Madge's voice rise in that certain way it did when she'd just made a sale, Evelyn's cackle from the workroom. Sounds she'd been hearing for four years. Sounds she'd become accustomed to, that usually made her smile.

Today they didn't. Today, all she could think about was how cool Mike Kwan had been to her, both this morning at his office, and then here, when he met with Brianna. How much it shouldn't bother her and how much it did.

And how completely confused she was.

Seated at the big desk, Brianna picked up the photo again, studying it with her typical quiet intensity. Then, with a soft, musical laugh, she sank back against the chair and shook her head. "I have to admit, Zo—the guy's good. Okay, you can tell your Mr. Kwan we're on."

Zoe nearly choked. "Ohhh, no, you don't," she said, waving both hands in front of her face. "That man is not *my* anything."

Brianna lifted one eyebrow, a hint of a smile playing around her lips. "Even though you were in cahoots with him about this?"

"That was different."

"Oh?"

"I know that look, Bree. Forget it. This was…" She heard herself echo Mike's words. "…strictly business."

"Mmm-hmm."

"Cut it out, lady," Zoe warned. "I go through enough head

games with my family—don't you start, too. Look, after listening to his schpiel, I decided he could probably do some really good things for the business, okay? That's it. So what if he is pushy and arrogant.'' She shrugged. ''I…liked what he had to say. I thought you should give him a shot.''

''Well…'' Brianna pushed herself up out of her chair. ''I could care less about his…character traits, as long as he gets the job done and stays on budget. But that's your department, not mine.''

Zoe's heart rocketed into her throat. ''What do you mean, *my* department?''

''Hey—you got him the job, right?'' Brianna grinned as she pulled a tortoiseshell comb out of her purse and ran it through her hair. ''You can deal with him. I've got far too much on my plate right now, anyway.'' She dropped the comb back into the purse, clicked it shut. ''I have complete faith in you. Which reminds me—did you get those prices on that watered silk for Bunny Andersen's gown?''

Out of nowhere, Zoe wondered what Brianna's reaction would be if she said ''No''. Shock? Anger? Disappointment? What if, for once, she hadn't done what was expected of her?

''Zo?'' Brianna's brows were lifted in mild curiosity. ''I'm sorry, kiddo—did you hear me? I need the pricing on the silk so I can give her a quote when she comes in tomorrow.''

But, of course, she had.

Zoe walked over to the desk and picked up a folder from the standing file behind the phone, flipped through a couple of pages, then read, ''Thirty-five dollars a yard. If you buy a whole bolt, they'll lower the price to $27.50.''

''Twenty-seven-fifty?'' Brianna waved her hand. ''Call them back. Remind them about the five-hundred-yard *peau de soie* order I just placed. Tell them $25 and it's a deal.''

In spite of herself, Zo grinned. Haggling was one of her favorite activities, ranking right up there with eating an entire mushroom-and-black-olive pizza all by herself and long soaks in the tub. ''Oh, Mr. Weitzer is gonna love this. I can hear it now.'' She clutched the front of her sweater. '''*Oy,* sweetheart—you're killin' me here. Just take my right arm, *bubelah*. It wouldn't hurt so much.' "

At that, Brianna lost it, laughing so hard she had to sit back down. "Oh my God, Zoe—you sound *exactly* like him." She wiped her eyes with the ends of her fingers.

"Yeah, well, I do a mean Mrs. Schiatterelli from B and T's Trims, too." She plopped the folder back into the file. "Wanna hear?"

But Brianna shook her head, still giggling. "I don't dare." Then she paused. "I'm going to miss you, you know."

Zoe's head snapped up. "Miss me? What are you talking about?"

"When you leave." Her employer stood up, then walked over and lifted her ivory wool swing coat off the coat tree near the door, slipped it on. She glanced at Zoe, then gave a short laugh. "You look shocked. Did you think I haven't thought about this? I don't expect you to hang around forever, you know."

Zoe could hardly piece together the fragments of her brain. "What makes you think I'm going anywhere, Brianna? I love this job—"

"I know you do, honey," she said, crossing back to Zoe. "But things change. People change." She shrugged, then slipped her purse strap onto her shoulder. As she worked her driving gloves onto her fingers, she fixed Zoe with a slight squint, the expression etching tiny creases around her mossy eyes. "Something tells me you're about ready for a change in your life, Zo. I have no idea *what,* but you've been rumbling around here like a volcano about to erupt." She reached over and gave Zoe's wrist a brief squeeze. "Just don't fight it, honey. Sometimes the very things we think we least want turn out to be exactly what we need."

Stunned, Zoe watched her boss walk to the office door, where she turned and said, almost as an afterthought, "It's all too easy to play these little games with ourselves, thinking we can save ourselves from being hurt. Unfortunately, if we don't risk getting hurt, we risk never being really happy, either. Just…think about it, okay?''

After Brianna left, Zoe wandered over to the large window overlooking the side yard, scanning the flower beds full of dead annuals she hadn't yet bothered to pull up. At least now that it was colder, she didn't have to make excuses for the struggling garden. She definitely liked winter gardens, she reflected, since they didn't require any effort on her part to keep going. She was tired of planting things, only to watch them inevitably die.

But then, she realized with a frown, if she stopped planting altogether, nothing would *ever* grow.

The phone rang. Mike pounced on it, grumbled something close to "Hello."

"Mr. Kwan?"

Seated in front of his computer at home, Mike crooked the phone into his aching neck, rubbing the space between his eyes. Stiff shouldered, grouchy and fed up with phones and interruptions, he'd grabbed his laptop and several clients' files and left work early, giving Fran explicit instructions that he wasn't to be disturbed unless it was an emergency. And even then, he'd said, she'd better think long and hard before calling.

Desperately searching his brain for what—*what*—could possibly have gone wrong in the half hour since he'd left, and who was this anyway, since it obviously wasn't Fran, his response was probably more curt than it should have been.

"Yes?"

"It's Zoe Chan…. Fran said—"

"Zoe?" His hand fell to the desk. "How did you get my number?"

On the other end, he heard a sigh that was more exasperation than patience. "I was about to say, when you interrupted me, that your assistant told me I could reach you here."

"Oh, of course."

Another sigh, then, unemotionally, "Brianna said yes. You've got the account."

He leaned back in his desk chair, forcing a stream of air through his lips. Figured. Now that he wasn't even sure he wanted it. Oh, it was still a good account, even though it wasn't going to bring in the big bucks he'd at first thought it might. Or even the prestige, if Brianna Fairchild stuck to her guns about not using her husband's name.

None of that mattered, not really. But Zoe Chan—and his attraction to her—did.

An attraction that nothing seemed to dampen—not knee-jerk reactions or cold shoulders or feigned indifference. It was as if something kept nagging him to search deeper, not to accept just what he saw on the surface, to give her a chance to show him who she really was. Yet, whenever he tried to envision what his potential relationship might be with this sloe-eyed spitfire, nothing seemed to fit.

Colleague? Friend? Lover? Mortal enemy?

"Have you heard one word I've been saying to you, Mr. Kwan?" speared through his thoughts.

Bet he knew which would be Zoe's choice.

"Oh, sorry. Got distracted."

"Hmm. Anyway, I suppose we need to meet about this campaign."

Any more tension in her voice and the phone wires would crack. He chuckled. "You needn't worry. They revoked my license to practice dentistry."

"Very funny. Well?"

He leaned forward on the desk, absently wiping dust off the computer screen, then jumped off the edge of a cliff he hadn't even realized he'd been near. "How about tonight? Over dinner?"

Her sigh was loud enough to make him lift the phone from his ear. "I don't do that, Mr. Kwan."

"Do what? Eat?"

"Have dinner. With a capital *D*."

"You mean, you have never in your life had dinner with a man in a restaurant?"

"Of course I've had dinner with a man in a restaurant.

That's not what I mean—oh, hell. Why am I wasting my breath?''

He grinned into the phone. "Doesn't sound wasted to me."

"Tomorrow at two," she said, clearly ignoring him. "I can come to your office or you can come to the salon."

On the screen he opened his appointment keeper and clicked on the next day. "Two looks good," he said. "Can I order in lunch?"

"You never give up, do you? Look," she said patiently, as if talking to someone's else's child, "no dinner, no lunch, nothing. I don't even want to see a bowl of mints on your desk when I get there, do you hear me?"

"Can I at least offer you coffee? Or do you consider that harassment, as well?"

"From you," she said, "a stick of gum could be construed as harassment."

He leaned back, crooking his arm around the back of his head. The woman might be prickly, but she was fun. She got—and kept—his juices going, kept him on his toes, made him laugh. "Okay. Two o'clock, no ingestible substances in sight. Agreed?"

"Fine. See you then. Oh…and by the way—" She stopped. "Yes?"

He heard her suck in a breath. "Since we're going to be working together, I need to clear the air about something. I…apologize for what I said the other day. About your being obnoxious. I was…" She cleared her throat. "I was overreacting."

He cradled the phone against his cheek. "Why?" he asked softly, realizing he was stroking the mouthpiece as if she could feel his caress.

"Let's…let's not get into the whys, okay? Just accept the apology and be grateful. I don't give them very often."

He felt his lips curve into a wry smile. "I don't imagine you do. Should I feel honored?"

"Don't push it," she said, then hung up.

* * *

Even in her first-thing-in-the-morning funk the day before, Zoe had been impressed with Mike's office. Older but respectable office building, gold-lettered The Kwan Agency on the glass door. Charcoal walls with blow-ups of magazine ads here and there, recessed lighting, silvery Berber carpeting, black lacquer reception desk, a half dozen carmine upholstered chairs in the waiting area in front of a simple brass-and-glass coffee table. Good view from the picture window behind the desk.

Today, on her second visit, she had to admit it was perfect. Striking but not flashy, confident but not pretentious.

By contrast, the gently aged woman whose entire face smiled at Zoe's appearance seemed to belong in a room filled with antiques, faded Oriental rugs, and about a dozen cats.

Yet she, too, was perfect.

"Oh! Are you Miss Chan?" she asked almost breathlessly, then hopped up out of her seat, one arm outstretched, as if manning the refreshments table at a church social. Softly waved hair, neither long nor short and sort of a faded apricot, was more or less confined by a pair of plain gold barrettes. If she wore makeup, it was so subtle as to be invisible. Her blouse was relentlessly white, polyester, and would probably have been more attractive had she left the top two buttons undone. Her gray flannel skirt ended precisely below her knees; her black leather pumps were painfully unadorned. By contrast to the almost military nature of the outfit, the black lambswool cardigan that kindly covered most of the generous figure underneath seemed downright frivolous, with its full bishop sleeves and filigreed gold buttons.

"Fran Summers, Mike's assistant," the woman announced with a brief, startlingly strong handshake. "We've talked on the phone, but it's so nice to meet you in person. Mike's on a conference call at the moment. Can I get you something to drink? Ice tea? Mineral water—?"

Zoe wouldn't have been surprised if she'd offered tea cakes and scones, as well. Nor would she have been disappointed.

Having worked through lunch, her stomach now felt like a sinkhole. But all she said was, "Tea would be great, thanks."

After a nod, Fran bustled over to a small Euro-style refrigerator masquerading as a cabinet underneath a long shelf. "Lemon or raspberry?" she said into the refrigerator.

"Raspberry, please." As Zoe eyed the room, trying to ignore her rumbling stomach, she noticed a large table off to one side with several dozen toys spread out on it. She walked over to the table, picking up one of the toys, a standard-sized action figure like the ones little boys nagged their parents to buy for them. Except this one was an African-American. An African-American *woman*.

Fran brought over Zoe's tea, poured over ice in a large glass.

"Does your boss have many clients with kids?" Zoe asked as she took the glass.

"Oh, my…I really have no idea—oh! You mean the toys!" Fran's laugh floated over the table. "Of course I can see why you'd ask that, but no. These are product samples, actually. Mike left them out so everyone coming and going can interact with them. He says living with the product for a few days is the best way to go about marketing it. You know…if you touch it or see it—or, in some cases, hear it—long enough, eventually you can figure out how to sell it."

"Toys?"

"My heavens, yes. Toys, car dealers, restaurants, insurance agents—we handle anything that's not toxic, culturally offensive or illegal." She clasped her hands underneath her prodigious bosom, as if about to launch forth in song. "These were developed," she said, pride coloring her words, "by a single mother whose son loves playing with toys like these. It occurred to her that it might be nice if he could play with some that looked like *him*, if you get my drift. And then she thought that maybe girls might like to play with something other than preposterously shaped fashion dolls. So she drew up some designs, took out a second mortgage on her house and found a manufacturer willing to make up a few thousand. Then she took them around to toy stores herself to sell them. Mike saw an interview with her on some local TV show, called her up and asked if she'd be interested in some free marketing advice—''

Zoe's eyes went wide at that. "Free?"

"Oh, yes," Fran said, nodding. Then she whispered, "We call these clients his 'strays'—tiny businesses he finds like bright pennies on the sidewalk. He takes the owners aside, gives them some advice, usually ends up getting them signed on.''

"I see," Zoe said with a smirk. "And then bills them."

"Well, not at first, of course, because they have no money. But usually by the end of six months, the campaign starts paying off.''

This was not what she expected to hear. "You mean, he carries his accounts?''

"Oh, just a few, now and again. Just those that have the right potential." Fran's glowing smile was the sort reserved by doting aunts for their favorite nephews. "Since life doesn't always like to play fair, Mike likes to level the field from time to time. Give the underdog an opportunity he—or she—" Fran picked up one of the toys and waved it for emphasis "—might not otherwise get. And it's extremely rare that the client, and Mike, aren't making money in short order. I tell you…he's got a lot of grateful clients who wouldn't have had a chance in hell if someone like Mike hadn't been willing to take a chance on them—"

Her intercom buzzed, cutting her off. She crossed to the desk, immediately offering Zoe another one of the those Mrs. Santa smiles. "Mike's waiting for you. Just go right on inside.…"

Zoe cast a last look at the array of multicultural toys before letting Fran show her into Mike's office. The instant the door opened, she thought she smelled pastrami and pickles. And French fries.

"Miss Chan! Please forgive the mess," he said, standing and wiping his fingers on a napkin. "I had to work straight through lunch.'' She tried—oh, did she try!—not to notice the grin sliding across his features. ''This is the first chance I've had to get to it. I...hope you don't mind...?''

Oh, God. Her nose had been right. Pastrami, French fries, a dill pickle...her salivary glands went into overdrive as her stomach began to chant ''Gimmegimmegimme....''

''Of course not,'' she said, gesturing toward the veritable banquet. ''Go right ahead.''

Slug.

''I'd offer you something,'' he said, ''but I know how you feel about that sort of thing—''

Jerk.

''Please—'' he gestured toward the chair on her side of the desk ''—have a seat.''

She did, edging the chair back a few inches as she folded her hands tightly across her pitifully empty tummy. Here she'd just about decided, based on Fran's comments, that Mike had some redeeming features. Some major redeeming features that warranted serious consideration.

Then he goes and pulls *this.*

He sat again, as well. He picked up a lidded cup off his blotter, took a pull from the straw, then held it up as if inspecting a fine piece of art. ''You ever have one of Woodside Deli's chocolate shakes, Miss Chan?''

''No,'' she said, swallowing. ''Can't say that I have.''

''They still make them right in front of you, on one of those old-fashioned milkshake makers with the big silver cups. So there's still chocolate syrup left in the bottom of the cup when you're finished.'' He tossed her a grin. ''You like chocolate?''

''Sometimes,'' she said through pursed lips, deciding she wouldn't mind watching him *drown* in one of his precious chocolate shakes.

He chuckled. Then had the nerve to take a huge chunk out of the pastrami sandwich.

''That stuff's not good for you, you know,'' she couldn't resist pointing out. ''Might as well just shoot up with lard.''

He shook his head. ''This is smoked turkey, lean. Lots of

spice, very little fat.'' He held out the sandwich. "Here, try it. It's delicious.''

She pushed herself back in the chair. "No, thank you.''

"Oh, right. I forgot. You equate offers of food with sexual advances.''

"What?''

"Our conversation yesterday, remember? Men offering you food can only mean one thing, right? Like reversing the Adam and Eve story—take a bite out of my sandwich and you get kicked straight out of the garden of propriety.'' He waved the sandwich around. Like a damn cape in front of a bull. "I got your message, loud and clear. So…take a look at this instead.…''

He wiped his hands again, then pushed a laminated report folder toward her full of proposals and costs and what all. She leafed through it, trying to concentrate on what she was reading. Her stomach, however, had other ideas.

"This, uh, looks fine.''

"That's it? *This looks fine?*''

She lifted her eyes. Was it her imagination, or was his tray of French fries closer than she remembered?

"What else am I supposed to say?''

"You're not going to argue with me, or tell me—in that particularly charming way you have—that I have a screw loose?''

She watched him for a second, trying to figure out—no, just trying to keep from reacting to—his damned twinkling eyes. The way *just* the corners of his mouth tugged up in a smile. That cleft in his chin—

Yanking her eyes back down to the report, she skimmed through it again, searching for something to argue about. Anything to keep him from thinking what he was clearly already thinking, which was that she was…

What?

Well, for crying out loud—how the hell should she know what Mike Chan was thinking about her? And why should she care?

She wiggled a bit in her chair, then shrugged. "You're staying within budget, as far as I can tell. I have to admit—this all looks fine. Except…" She glanced up. "What sort of direct mailing do you have in mind? We were planning to send out invitations anyway to several hundred retailers."

He seemed to study her for a moment, sucking on his straw. She caught herself licking her lips.

"I'll show you what I had in mind," he said, his mouth twitching at the corners, then turned away for a second to pull something out of the filing cabinet behind his desk.

She snatched three fries and crammed them into her mouth.

"What do you think of these?" He spun back around, an array of colorful brochures in his hand. One brow slid up. "Is…something wrong, Miss Chan?"

Her mouth full, all she could manage was a quick shake of her head. If she chewed, or swallowed, *he'd know*. And, natch, the man wouldn't take his eyes off her.

Then—thank you, Lord!—she remembered her tea. Keeping her French-fry-stuffed mouth still, she brought the glass to her pooched-out lips and took a sip, hoping she wouldn't choke on the half-chewed potatoes as they scraped down her throat. After as delicate a swallow as she could manage under the circumstances, she held out her hand for the brochures. Mike handed them to her, his eyes dancing with what she supposed was amusement.

She tried to speak. Mistake number one.

"These—" A wad of raspberry-drenched spud threatened to blow her cover. Her eyes tearing from the effort not to choke, she swallowed again. The brochures undulated beneath her blurry eyes, the colors all swimming together. "These look…great," she rasped.

"Zoe?"

Blinking madly, she looked up. "What?" she said in a small voice.

Mike leaned forward in his chair, his hands folded together in front of him on his blotter. "Just eat the damn French fries, already. I promise I won't read anything untoward into it, okay?''

She took a deep breath, which was mistake number two, because she started choking all over again. After another sip of tea, she said, more clearly this time, ''I have no idea what you're talking ab—''

His chuckle cut her off. ''I've been listening to your stomach growl for the past ten minutes.'' He leaned back in his chair, cupping the side of his face in his palm. ''Did you skip lunch, too?''

Finally she nodded.

He stood up, grabbing his suit jacket from the back of the chair. ''Let's go.''

''Excuse me?''

Before she could protest further, however, he had taken her by the elbow and gently lifted her to her feet. ''The deli makes fabulous vanilla shakes, too, if you'd prefer.''

Zoe pulled back, for a moment, every instinct telling her to not give in. Not yet. Not ever.

Mike had walked away a few feet; now he turned back, one brow quirked. ''Well?''

This was wrong.

This was nothing.

This was…a mess.

''Chocolate is fine,'' she said, following him. But when he reached out to take her arm, she pulled away, crossing her arms so tightly over her rib cage, she made her stomach growl again.

5

At this time of day, the crowd had thinned out to a manageable crush. Still, Mike had some skillful maneuvering to do to get them a booth. A waiter handed them menus the size of billboards, then vanished as if washed overboard.

Mike looked over to say something to Zoe, only to find himself faced with a foot-and-a-half-high wall of laminated cardboard covered with pictures of cheesecake and blintzes. He tucked two fingers over the edge of the menu, pulled it down. She looked up, annoyed.

"What?"

"I can't see you."

"Tough," she said, yanking the menu away from him and *thwacking* the end back down on the tabletop. "You brought me here to eat," he heard from behind the menu, "so no conversation until I've decided what."

Such a gracious date, he mused. "Well, that's a step in the right direction."

She lowered the menu just enough to peer over it. "What's that supposed to mean?"

"If I'm interpreting your comments correctly—which I realize is treading on dangerous ground—you're saying that there will be conversation. At some point."

Back up went the menu. "Maybe."

The waiter returned; Mike ordered coffee. Zoe ordered lentil soup, a Reuben on rye, fries and a chocolate shake.

Then followed one of those horrible silences when you can clearly hear every word the people behind you are saying.

The waiter brought them a basket filled with little packages of crackers; Zoe rattled through the choices for several seconds, which at least muffled the painfully detailed description of somebody's Aunt Zelda's gallbladder operation, finally selecting a package of garlic-flavored melba toast. She ripped open the cellophane and dumped out her booty onto a napkin.

"You can stand that stuff?" he asked.

"It's food. It's here. I'm hungry." She bit off half of one cracker, mumbling around it, "So sue me."

He braced his forearms on the edge of the table and leaned forward, his hands loosely clasped in front of him. "I bet you can't name three places you'd rather be less right now."

Her jaw stopped in midchew. Never taking her eyes off him, she swallowed, took a sip of water and swallowed again. "Than here, you mean?"

"Mmm-hmm."

"Sure I can," she said. "My mother's. Any Chinese restaurant. My gynecologist's."

With a short laugh, he leaned back again, crossing his arms over his chest. "I understand the first one. And can surmise about the third. But the second one's got me over a barrel. You don't like Chinese food?"

"Great subject for the next Sally Jesse, don't you think? *Women who can't stand their own ethnic cuisine.*" She stuffed most of the second cracker into her mouth.

"*And the men who love them,*" he said before he thought about it.

All she could do was glare, since her mouth was filled. But that was enough.

"Sorry," he said, not sure he really was. "Just slipped out."

"Forget it," she mumbled as the waiter set her food in front of her.

They spoke in circles for several minutes after that, while Mike watched this woman who couldn't possibly weigh more than ninety-five pounds put away a bigger lunch than he had. As her stomach filled, though, her mouth loosened.

And they were talking. *To* each other, not *at* each other.

They discussed the weather—she thought it would rain later; he didn't—over soup. Term limits—she was for, he against—between bites of the enormous sandwich. Whether film critics should be heeded or ignored, whether certain books benefited or suffered from being made into movies, how much caffeine was too much. They argued, with soft-edged intensity, sometimes both talking at the same time. They agreed, more than he thought they would, but when they didn't, they listened to each other.

First-date stuff, he realized, a little amazed by what was happening. Quasi-serious, edging on controversial but not close enough to stifle further exploration.

Interesting.

She was slowing down. There were still French fries left, and she hadn't eaten one in several seconds. As if reading his mind, she pushed the plate over to him with a short, self-conscious thrust.

"Help yourself," she said. "I shouldn't have eaten the melba toast."

He grinned down at the place mat, looked back up at her. She seemed almost relaxed. Almost. "Does that mean you don't want dessert?"

"Bite your tongue," she said, nodding toward the dessert case in the back. "If I have to be carted out, I'm not leaving without a piece of that cheesecake."

He caught the waiter's eye, ordered the cheesecake.

"So…what do you do when you're not Brianna Fairchild's assistant?"

She eyed him thoughtfully for a long moment, then asked, "Why?"

"Because I want to know."

"Why?" she repeated.

"Anyone ever tell you that you ask too many questions?"

"Anyone ever tell you that you tend to be devious?"

"Tend to be?" he responded with a chuckle. "If I can believe some of the tales my mother tells me about my childhood, deviousness was my primary characteristic."

"I can believe it." She leaned her chin in her hand and gave a loud sigh. "What do I do when I'm not working?" She shrugged. "Watch videos, burn microwave dinners, read long convoluted trashy novels, kill plants and go on dates from hell."

"That paints a pretty clear picture," he said, amazed at her sudden candor.

"Mm. I thought it might. Oh—one more thing. Avoid my sisters."

"Your sisters? Why?"

"I have two. Margi's one year older, Vanessa's two. Both married. Margi, in fact, is due to have her first child next month. Anyway, they—along with my mother—have made it their life mission to see me 'settled.' Which translates into making my life miserable."

"I see. Hence, the dates from hell?"

"Exactly."

The cheesecake arrived. Zoe studied it for a moment, picked up her fork, sighed and dived in.

"So…" she said around her dessert, "in order to preserve my sanity, I avoid them as much as possible. In fact—" she leaned forward with a conspiratorial gleam in her eyes "—I just got them off my case about going out with some man they met at a Chinese restaurant."

"Oh…really?"

"Yeah. You know the Golden Dragon? Oh, of course you do. We met there the other night. Well, apparently old Mr. Wu has a grandson whom my sisters have determined is just what I need."

"Really?" he said again.

"Mm. But—" she waved a bite of cheesecake around as she spoke "—I told them no way, José. This woman is not going out with any more losers."

Swallowing a smile, Mike palmed his chin in his hand. "And what makes you think the guy's a loser?"

"They all are," she said in a so-that's-that voice, plunking her fork down on the empty plate. "Blind dates are God's way for getting you back for every rotten thing you did—or thought about doing—as a little kid. I'm sure of it."

Food, apparently, was the magic potion that warmed her up and softened her defenses. "So what about you?" she now asked.

His chin lifted off his palm. "Me?"

"Yeah. You dug into my personal life, such as it is." She wiped her mouth with her napkin. "So it's my turn to be nosy. What do you do besides work?"

"Think about work."

She reminded him of a small bird, with her quick, constant movement. And, like a bird, her occasional periods of stillness were purposeful and intense. In one of those periods now, she met his gaze, the napkin clutched in her fingers. "Do you...go out much?"

Was she fishing? Or just being polite? "Occasionally. It never pans out, though."

Her brows dipped. "Why?"

He thought carefully about his answer, not sure what message he wanted to send. Decided to simply tell the truth. "Because, after innumerable disasters, I've finally realized there's no room in my life for a woman. I'm not around enough to give a woman the kind of attention she deserves." He watched for her reaction. There didn't seem to be one. "I doubt I'll ever marry."

If he hadn't been watching so carefully, he would have missed the slight, momentary widening of her eyes. "Know what you mean," she then said, looking away as she lay her napkin by her plate, slipped her cardigan back on, gathered up her purse. Making herself busy again. "Don't see matrimony in my future either," she tossed off. "But try to tell my sisters that!"

He stood first, then automatically held out his hand to help her out of the booth. To his surprise, she simply took it. No comments, no arguments, no snide grimaces.

It was harder than he realized it would be to let go.

"So you really hate Chinese food?" he asked, picking up the check. He noticed that she let him, again without argument. "Why? Your parents in the restaurant business?"

"What? Oh, no." He grinned. "My parents aren't even in the country."

Zoe went back to work, secured the caterer for the Mitchell-O'Malley wedding and the florist for the Yamaguchi-Mac-Pherson's, helped Renee Harrison pick out a gown, guided Nancy through some tricky paperwork she hadn't seen before, walked into her office, sat down and thought about that lunch.

In spite of herself, she'd had a good time. Certainly a helluva lot better time than she'd had on the past half-dozen "dates" combined. And...well, okay. Might as well admit it: she liked Mike. Really, truly liked him. He listened to what she had to say, and what *he* had to say was interesting enough to listen *to*. While he could be irreverent, which was fine, he was still a gentleman, which was better. And as far as she could tell, postnasal drip was not a problem.

And there he was, not in the least bit interested in having a relationship. She'd finally met someone smart and nice and generous and attractive, even, and he was already married to his work.

Didn't that just beat all?

Mike returned to the office about four, having run several errands after lunch, to find his assistant sitting with a goofy expression on her face.

"What's with you? You look like your girdle's too tight."

Fran ignored him. As usual. "She's the 'too,' isn't she?"

"Huh?" You'd think, after three years, he'd be pretty good at following Fran's sometimes convoluted conversational paths, but this one stumped him. "The 'too'?"

"As in, 'Do you hate me, *too?*'"

God, the woman had a brain like a bear trap. Of course, that's what made her invaluable in an office that ran on a trillion details. But that's also why she made him crazy. Crazier.

He could hedge. Hell, he could downright lie. Wouldn't do him a bit of good.

"Yes," he admitted, "but—"

She held up one hand, then returned her attention to whatever it was she was working on. "I didn't ask for, nor do I want to know, the objections as to why this one won't work. Or listen to the same tale of woe I've been listening to ad nauseam about your inability to sustain a relationship or why you're not good marriage material or whatever the excuse is this week." Now she raised slitted, suspicious cat's eyes to him. "It's all bull pucky, and you know it. Using work as an excuse not to get involved is the oldest trick in the book."

"It's not an excuse, Fran—"

"Like hell it isn't," she muttered, checking off some list or other. "This may come as a bit of a surprise, since I hide my age so well—" she flipped over the page, began skimming the next "—but I wasn't born yesterday. And I've raised three sons to adulthood. I know all the lines. Hell—a man would use the fact that it's Monday and he was wearing the wrong pair of shoes if he thought he could get away with it."

Now she gave him her full attention, putting down her pen and clasping her hands in front of her. He felt like a kid being chided by the principal for putting a frog in the teacher's desk. "I don't believe, for one single solitary minute, that anyone *really* wants to come home to an empty house every night, that work can possibly substitute for a warm body to share your bed with or someone to watch late-night television with or watch a rosebush blossom with. What are you afraid of, Michael?"

Mike tried to ignore the taut muscles at the base of his neck. "You've been watching too many greeting-card commercials, Fran," he said. "Life's not a fairy tale. And anyway—"

"It's not a blank page, either, Michael." She rose as well, coming around to the front of the desk to clasp her hands on his arms. "You're too damn young to chuck it all, to give up trying to find your soul mate—"

"Oh, please, Fran," he said with a dry laugh. "Spare me the 'soul mate' routine. Besides—"

"Fine. Call it whatever you want. Just don't shut yourself off."

His sigh sailed over her head, then he glanced down into her face. "Fran…"

She let go of his arms and walked back around her desk, settling herself back in. "I've said my piece," she said, adjusting her glasses on her nose. "But just consider this, would you—you spend twelve hours a day thinking about how to make other people's lives better, how to make other people's dreams come true. Spend at least *some* of the remaining twelve thinking about how to make *your* life better, okay?"

Angrier than he wanted to be, though he doubted his irritation was directed entirely at his assistant, he stormed into his office. His hand caught the door, preparing to slam it, when he made the mistake of trying to get in the last word.

"This business *is* my life, Fran. And if I neglect it, a lot of other people's lives will be in the lurch, too."

"Oh, give me a break, Michael," Fran said, almost wearily, before twisting herself in her chair to peer at him over her glasses. "You'd be surprised just how well we could manage without you from time to time."

Then he slammed the door.

"And if you don't stop slamming the damn door," came Fran's crackly voice over the intercom on the corner of his desk, "you leave me no choice but to believe I'm right."

Fran *was* right, of course. Work would never substitute for a relationship. No matter how much he wanted to believe that, since he couldn't seem to make a relationship work, he didn't need one. And, were it not for Zoe Chan's intrusion into his life, perhaps the blinders wouldn't have slipped off quite so soon.

Damn her.

Mike collapsed into the chair behind his desk, swiveling it around so he could take in the view north, up Peachtree toward Buckhead. He had a hundred things he should be doing. Calls to return, budgets to analyze, material to approve. So here he sat, staring out the window, thinking about Zoe.

And admitting to himself, at long last, how incredibly lonely he was.

He'd enjoyed lunch, a hundred times more than he'd thought he would. If nothing else, he thought she'd make a good friend. But he was deluding himself if he thought that's *all* he wanted.

Mike played back their conversation in his head, trying to remember her facial expressions, her body language, when she talked about her work and her miserable dating experience. Like him, work was her life. But he sensed she wasn't entirely happy with that.

She wasn't entirely happy, period. But he wasn't the person to make it better. Couldn't be that person, even if he wanted to be. Zoe Chan needed more than he could offer. She needed someone who would be there for her, who could shower her with the attention she needed. Deserved. And, he suspected, *craved*, although he'd bet his right arm she'd have to be tied to the stake with the flames licking at her feet before she'd admit it.

In the next month alone, he had trips scheduled for Chicago, San Francisco, Toronto, some small town in Mississippi he couldn't even remember the name of, New York. Garnering new clients, taking care of old ones. Sure, faxes and E-mail and phone calls could handle much of it, but that wasn't Mike's way. To his way of thinking, it wasn't personal enough.

His gaze lit on the brochure samples he'd meant for her to take, as well as the outline of the campaign. When he picked them up, he could smell her perfume.

His fist closed around the edge of the paper as his breath left his lungs in a ragged, frustrated sigh. This time, however, things could get *too* personal.

Maybe he had used work as an excuse. But now that he'd set certain wheels in motion, he couldn't change them just because they might no longer mesh with his personal agenda. Wanting things to be different didn't mean they could be.

Foolishly he lifted the brochures to his nose, inhaled her scent. And swore.

He'd have a messenger take the things up to Fairchild's. From now on, as much as possible, other people in the office could handle the account.

It really was best this way. For everyone.

6

In the three weeks since Zoe had gone mall-waddling with Margi—and since she'd last laid eyes on Mike Kwan—she hadn't seen her sisters at all. By her choice. Actually, other than the occasional I've-got-to-run-but-just-wanted-to-check-to-see-how-you-were-doing phone calls, she hadn't even talked to them. There had been no further attempts to fix her up, with David Wu's grandson or anybody else. Even her mother had been more reticent than usual on the subject. Naively, she thought she was home free.

But then, this was the child who'd clung to her belief in Santa Claus until she was nearly ten years old.

Then, one Friday evening in early October, Zoe heard the back doorbell ring. Insistently. In a state of contented dishabille, she padded down the back stairs in her flannel jammies and scuffs to find her sisters waiting for her.

"Brother, you do lead an exciting life," Vanessa said, rolling her eyes. "Pj's at seven. Wildwoman strikes again."

Zoe crossed her arms and leaned against the doorjamb. "So how do you know I'm not entertaining a man in my apartment?"

The sisters looked at each other and burst out laughing.

"Honey, if that's the sort of thing you wear to entertain a man," Vanessa said, pushing her way past Zoe, "you're in far worse shape than I thought."

"I second that," Margi said, plodding in behind her sister, her trench coat gaping open around an oversize green sweater that made her look like a walking watermelon. She eyed Zoe's disreputable attire and shook her head. "Sheesh, Zo—I don't let myself look *that* bad. Even now."

"So now that you've thoroughly humiliated me and cast aspersions on my attire—attire which, may I point out, I wear in the privacy of my own home and for no one's comfort or convenience except my own—what are you two doing here? And where are your husbands?"

Out of deference to the overripe Margi, who didn't look any too thrilled about the prospect of climbing the flight of stairs to Zoe's apartment, they landed in the waiting room. Vanessa clicked on a couple of lamps, then helped Margi onto one of the love seats.

"Oh, gee, Marg, maybe…" Zoe hesitated, gnawing on her knuckle.

"What?" Margi asked.

"Don't you dare let your water break or I'm in deep doo-doo."

"Oh, for crying out loud, Zo—I'm not due for another month. Stick a sock in it."

Zoe stuck her tongue out at her, then flopped into one of the wicker chairs, tucking her feet up under her. "So? Husbands?"

"Harry's at a hot penny ante poker game out in Decatur," Vanessa said, picking nonexistent lint off her black wool slacks, "and Scott's out of town until Wednesday."

"Out of town? What's this all about?" Zoe looked to Margi, who was shifting uncomfortably on the love seat, stuffing throw pillows behind her back.

"His new job," she explained through a cross between a grunt and a sigh. "They've expanded his territory, so he has to be out of town two weeks a month."

"Oh, yuck." Zoe leaned forward, taking her sister's hand. "What about when the baby's due?"

Margi shook her head, seemingly unconcerned. "Not a problem. He's got the week off before and after the due date, so we're covered—"

"Listen," Vanessa interrupted. "We're not here to talk about Scott's carousing around the Georgian countryside. Get dressed. We're going out to dinner."

"Which I already had. Sorry."

"Tough. You can eat again," Margi said. "Or you can watch *me* eat. I could care less. But I didn't drag my carcass all this way to stay here and watch TV." After a try or two, she hefted herself off the couch. "So go get dressed. We made reservations at Caraveggio's."

Zoe's eyes darted from one to the other as visions of scampi danced in her head.

"Caraveggio's?"

Vanessa grinned at Margi. "Told you that would get her." They gave each other a high five.

Zoe headed for the staircase. "Be right back," she said as she ran up the stairs. "Don't leave without me."

Truth was, she was just as glad to get out of the house and away from her thoughts, which had been pee-poor company the past couple of days. In spite of how busy she had been these last few weeks, she wasn't too busy to notice Mike Kwan's absence. He'd apparently relegated much of the campaign to his staff, which was understandable, certainly, and efficient, and good business sense. He'd been away a lot, too, according to Fran. Dodging a late-season hurricane in Mississippi, last she'd heard.

Oh, she knew it was dumb to think about him so much. He'd made it perfectly clear he wasn't interested in a relationship, that his work came first. She'd finally reconciled herself that what she'd misconstrued as flirting, maybe the seed of a romantic interest, was nothing more than Mike being Mike: outgoing, friendly, a pal. Still, *hope* sat huddled in a corner of her heart like a child waiting to be sprung from "time-out." Every once in a while, it would squirm and call out in a tiny voice, *"Can I come out yet?"* And she would have to sigh and say, "Not yet," afraid to admit that maybe it would have to stay inside her, cramped and forsaken, forever.

All this bunk she'd tried to make herself believe about not needing a man... Well, perhaps, on some level, it was still true. She didn't need a man to survive. Or to feel complete. Or even, she supposed, to be happy. If she thought about it that way, she didn't *need* a man at all.

But what happened when you saw one you just plain out-and-out *wanted?* Then what?

So. Here she sat in a crowded Italian restaurant in Buckhead, an inch away from no-holds-barred self-pity, having dinner with her sisters. A pair of Cantonese yentas.

What was she, nuts?

They got through the antipasto fine, and most of the main course, the conversation focusing mainly on Margi's pregnancy, family gossip, husbands' bad habits and Margi's pregnancy. Boring, predictable, safe. Zoe actually started to feel better.

"Guess who I ran into the other day?" Margi asked.

Somehow, Zoe knew the answer wasn't Auntie Rose. She instantly tensed, her fork suspended halfway to her mouth. At the next table, four waiters started a rousing version of "Happy Birthday."

"Who?" she shouted over the din, but she couldn't hear the first part of Margi's response. She squinted at her sister's moving lips, but couldn't make out the name.

"You know? David Wu's grandson?"

"Oh."

"Yeah... Sheesh!" Margi cast an annoyed glance over her shoulder at the noise, but simply leaned forward and kept going. "He's been in and out of town a lot on business—did I tell you he has his own business?"

The last words were lost in thunderous applause and shouts of approval for the birthday celebrant.

Zoe shook her head, trying to convince the bite of scampi in her mouth to go down her throat.

"What did you say he did, Marg?" Vanessa asked in the lull.

Another *hurrah* went up from the table as the person ap-

WELCOME TO THE
CASINO!

Try your luck at the Roulette Wheel ...
Play a hand of Twenty-One!

How to play:

1. Play the Roulette and Twenty-One scratch-off games, as instructed on the opposite page, to see that you are eligible for FREE BOOKS and a FREE GIFT!

2. Send back the card and you'll receive TWO brand-new Silhouette Yours Truly™ novels. These books have a cover price of $3.50 each, but they are yours to keep absolutely free.

3. There's no catch. You're under no obligation to buy anything. We charge nothing — ZERO — for your first shipment. And you don't have to make any minimum number of purchases — not even one!

4. The fact is, thousands of readers enjoy receiving books by mail from the Silhouette Reader Service™ before they're available in stores. They like the convenience of home delivery, and they love our discount prices!

5. We hope that after receiving your free books you'll want to remain a subscriber. But the choice is yours — to continue or cancel, any time at all!

So why not take us up on our invitation, with no risk of any kind. You'll be glad you did!

Play Twenty-One For This Exquisite Free Gift!

THIS SURPRISE
MYSTERY GIFT
COULD BE
YOURS FREE WHEN
YOU PLAY
TWENTY-ONE

It's fun, and we're giving away *FREE GIFTS* to all players!

PLAY ROULETTE!

Scratch the silver to see where the ball has landed—7 RED or 11 BLACK makes you eligible for TWO FREE romance novels!

PLAY TWENTY-ONE!

Scratch the silver to reveal a winning hand! Congratulations, you have Twenty-One. Return this card promptly and you'll receive a fabulous free mystery gift, along with your free books!

YES!

Please send me all the free Silhouette Yours Truly™ books and the gift for which I qualify! I understand that I am under no obligation to purchase any books, as explained on the back of this card.

Name (please print clearly)

Address _____ Apt.#

City _____ State _____ Zip

(U-SIL-YT-01/99)   201 SDL CKFN

The Silhouette Reader Service™ — Here's how it works:

Accepting free books places you under no obligation to buy anything. You may keep the books and gift and return the shipping statement marked "cancel." If you do not cancel, about a month later we'll send you 4 additional novels and bill you just $2.90 each, plus 25¢ delivery per book and applicable sales tax, if any.* That's the complete price — and compared to cover prices of $3.50 each — quite a bargain! You may cancel at any time, but if you choose to continue, every other month we'll send you 4 more books, which you may either purchase at the discount price...or return to us and cancel your subscription.
*Terms and prices subject to change without notice. Sales tax applicable in N.Y.

If offer card is missing write to: Silhouette Reader Service, 3010 Walden Ave., P.O. Box 1867, Buffalo, NY 14240-9952

BUSINESS REPLY MAIL
FIRST-CLASS MAIL   PERMIT NO 717   BUFFALO NY

POSTAGE WILL BE PAID BY ADDRESSEE

SILHOUETTE READER SERVICE
3010 WALDEN AVE
PO BOX 1867
BUFFALO NY 14240-9952

NO POSTAGE
NECESSARY
IF MAILED
IN THE
UNITED STATES

parently blew out the candles on the cake, wiping out Margi's answer, as well.

"Oh, right," Vanessa said. "I'd forgotten."

"Anyway," she said to Zoe, "he said he'd like to meet you."

"Oh, no," Zoe groaned, leaning her forehead in her hand.

"No, really. Whenever you like, he said."

It had been a long week. Her defenses were down. The scampi—and an indulgent glass of Chianti—had mellowed her out. And they wouldn't give up until she'd agreed. The sooner she did, the sooner she could get on with her life.

"Okay, okay, fine, whatever," she said, throwing her hands up in surrender. "After Market, I'll meet this guy." With any luck, Manhattan would topple over into the East River and she'd be off the hook. "On one condition—that we not talk about it any more this evening."

They both made murmuring sounds of approval, agreement and triumph.

Empty dinner plates were exchanged for three plates of brownies with vanilla ice cream and hot fudge sauce. Italian, no. Decadent, absolutely.

"You're not going to regret it. This guy is *fabulous*—"

"Margi?"

"What?" Wide, "who-me?" eyes met hers.

"Shut up."

With an unconcerned shrug, her sister changed the subject.

"Speaking of New York, when did you say you were leaving?" Vanessa asked, spooning in a glob of dessert.

"Next Friday," Zoe said. "We're going up on Spencer's jet."

"Well, ex-*cuse* me," Margi said, fanning herself. The front of the green sweater was now adorned with dribbles of marinara sauce. Then she laughed.

Immediately followed by a yelp.

"Baby kicking again?"

"I...don't know.... Ouch! *Ouch!*"

Zoe exchanged glances with Vanessa, then they both jumped out of their chairs.

"What is it?" "Is it the baby?" they said simultaneously.

"Well, it sure as hell ain't the marinara sauce doing this," Margi said, pressing her hand into the side of her belly.

Instantly the genial atmosphere in the restaurant exploded into near panic as both patrons and staff caught wind of what was happening. The owner flapped about like the proverbial headless chicken, fifty years of English completely forgotten in the heat of the moment. Zoe made out *"dottore,"* *"bambino,"* and a host of *"Dio mios"* as she and Vanessa maneuvered the now-panting Margi to her feet.

While Vanessa got Margi out to the car, Zoe took care of the bill and helped Vittorio retrieve his English.

"Sorry, Missa Chan. My wife, she have eight *bambini,* an' they comma out like bars of soap—*zhoop!*" This was accompanied by an amazingly descriptive pantomime. "So I see your sister, I think she gonna give birth right here inna *ristorante.*"

"It's okay," Zoe said, signing the Visa bill. Excitement or no, Vittorio wasn't too rattled to take care of *that.* "The hospital's just a few minutes away. She'll be fine."

As Zoe left the restaurant, Vittorio called out behind her, "You let me know what it is—girl or boy?"

"Sure thing," she called over her shoulder, giving him a thumbs-up.

What it was was a false alarm. A muscle cramp brought on by an overactive baby inside a tiny woman. That had set off a series of Braxton-Hicks contractions that, while strong, and frightening, were nowhere near the cervix.

Mortified, Margi sat on the emergency room examining table, glowering at her enormous middle. "And how am I supposed to know when they *are* near the cervix?"

The ER doctor grinned. "Oh, trust me. You'll know."

Margi raised one skeptical eyebrow, then held out an arm so Zoe could help her down.

"Sheesh. How to ruin a perfectly good evening," she muttered as she slowly made her way out of the examining area and down the hall, Zoe and Vanessa flanking her.

"Hey—I thought it was kind of fun, didn't you, Zo?"

"Oh, absolutely. Here I could have spent a dull evening watching the mating rituals of small jungle mammals on PBS or something. Instead, I got to act out *Speed* through downtown Atlanta in a ten-year-old Corolla."

Margi glanced at first one, then the other, then said, "Fine. Make fun of my misery. But just remember—one day, *you* guys will go through this, and I'll remember. And I'm going to— *Damn*." They had gotten as far as the entrance when she stopped to breathe through another Braxton-Hicks.

Zoe watched her sister's face and felt her own crumple. Margi really was miserable. And to have her husband away so much.... She didn't envy her one bit.

She really didn't, she realized as they settled Margi into the front seat of Vanessa's car. A part-time husband, a miserable pregnancy—who needed it? Certainly she didn't.

In silence, they took Margi home first, saw her to bed and told her five times each to call if she needed anything. Chastened by her recent experience, however, she shook her head.

"I won't bug you guys anymore," she said on a yawn. "After all, the doctor said it was only serious if one of two things happened—my water broke or it felt as if someone had set my crotch on fire." This was stated as calmly as though she was describing learning how to swim. Snuggling down into her pillows, her swollen belly propped on one of its own, she told them all to turn out the lights when they left and she'd talk to them tomorrow.

"So what's the point?" Zoe asked several minutes later in Vanessa's car, on the way back to her house.

"What's what point?" Vanessa asked.

"Marriage. Pregnancy. Babies."

In the darkness, Vanessa shot her a look of utter stupefaction. "You're kidding, right?"

"Why would I kid? Why would anyone go through that?"

It apparently took her sister a moment to gather her thoughts. "Maybe…because she's completely in love with her husband and she wants to have this baby? Like women have for thousands of years?"

"But she's miserable…"

"Of course she is. And she misses Scott, too, before you start in on that. But sometimes you gotta go through the miserables to get to the good parts, you know?" When Zoe didn't respond, Vanessa glanced at her again. "What's up with you, honey? Ever since your birthday, you've been…well, *weird*, if you really want to know."

"I don't."

"Well, tough. Someone's got to say this, and I guess I'm nominated. I just don't get it, Zo. You've always loved babies—look at how close you are to Brianna's kids. Now, suddenly, your own sister is pregnant, and you've become this big grouch. What gives?"

She did love Brianna's children, and took her honorary auntie role very seriously. But it was true. Her malaise from several weeks ago was getting worse. And everything, it seemed, good or bad, only served to exacerbate her perpetual foul mood.

And Michael Kwan was right at the top of the list.

She shrugged. "Maybe it's some sort of early midlife crisis," she suggested, hardly willing to go into what was really bothering her. "I have no idea. No idea what's wrong or what it would take to make 'it'—whatever 'it' is—better." She turned back to the window, deliberately softening her focus so that the neon signs and car lights all blurred into tangled ribbons as the car meandered its way back to the house.

"Has it ever occurred to you…?" Her sister hesitated.

"What?"

"Well, I know you're going to jump all over me, but it just seems that…" Vanessa flicked a glance in her direction. "I think you're lonely, honey. But you've been so busy since you got out of college you never even noticed—"

"Oh, don't be ridiculous—" But her eyes stung.

"No, I'm serious. I'm not saying there aren't people who really do prefer to be alone, but I honestly don't think you're one of them. Not for the long haul, anyway. And it's just taken this long for it to catch up with you. That's all. And now I'll shut up."

Zoe crossed her arms, staring straight ahead as they drove. "Thanks. I appreciate it."

But even though her sister's voice was silenced, the one inside her own head wasn't. And unfortunately, the two voices seemed to be agreeing with each other.

That last week before they left for Market was, to put it simply, insane. Mike had suggested that, to save money and time, they combine mailing the invitations to the New York show with the brochures, since they had no way of knowing which of the smaller shops' owners or buyers would actually make the trip to New York. Brianna and Zoe had agreed, which meant a marathon to get at least half the sample gowns photographed, for Mike's art department to design the brochure and to get it printed and mailed.

But everybody busted their buns to get it all done, and the mailing went out, and they no sooner had caught their collective breaths than the responses started pouring in.

The day before they were due to leave, Brianna and Zoe sat, somewhat stunned, in the office, surveying the mountain of mail and faxes and printed-out E-mails in front of them. RSVPs for the show, requests for more information or brochures, even several early orders.

"The man's a genius," Brianna said with a soft laugh. "Would you look at this?" She shook her head. "I'm blown away."

"What you are," Zoe said from her desk as she printed out the latest batch of E-mails, "is talented."

"And smart enough to let you talk me into signing on with your Mr. Kwan."

Zoe decided it was better not to respond to that.

"Who, I forgot to tell you, is flying up with us tomorrow."

That she responded to.

"Flying up with us? What on earth for?"

"Oh, he mentioned he had business in New York next week, so he'd be around if we needed to pick his brain. So I invited him to come up with us. He'll fly back Delta Thursday morning." Brianna slanted a glance at Zoe, then returned to opening the mail. "Why? You have a problem with his going with us?"

"Why should I have a problem with that?"

"I have no idea. But unless you've been to a tanning salon recently, you've just turned a very pretty shade of peach."

"It's the light," she countered, facing the computer screen. "It's nearly sunset."

"Mmm-hmm." Brianna leaned forward. "He's cute."

"Who's cute?"

"Your Mr. Kwan."

"He's not *my*..." She caught herself. "Honestly, lady..." She got up from her chair and smacked the batch of printouts into Brianna's outstretched hand. "Where do you get these ideas?"

"Oh...I'm just remembering a conversation we had, several years ago, about your instincts regarding someone who's since become very dear to me." She grinned. "I believe your words were 'a serious definite possibility.'"

"That was different."

"Why?"

To her annoyance, she felt the blush deepen. "Because Spencer...isn't an arrogant, overbearing turkey."

Brianna burst out laughing. "Boy, your memory must be worse than I thought. If I recall, we *both* thought *exactly* that!" She added the new printouts to one of the piles on her desk. "And if you expect me to believe that you think that about Mike Kwan, you must think I'm totally blind." The hazy green eyes assessed her for a moment, then added, "And something tells me he doesn't think you're so bad yourself."

Zoe's little *hope* poked at her. *"You hear that?"* it asked, in a voice that was becoming squeakier and more irritating every day.

"Oh, be quiet," she said to both of them at once.

He'd been on private jets before, but never in the company of a pair of overwrought toddlers. Or a woman who made his blood hum in his veins just by thinking about her.

Zoe was seated apart from the family, her laptop already set up and running. To her right sat a large stack of papers of assorted sizes, from which she was apparently entering information into the computer. She must have heard him come on board. But she hadn't even acknowledged his presence.

Hmm.

He'd run into Margi two nights ago at his grandfather's restaurant. Her announcement—a little breathless, he'd thought, but that might have been due to the pregnancy—that Zoe had agreed to "meet" him nearly blew him away.

But, unless he was way off base, the woman in front of him knew nothing about any of this.

As the Lockharts settled their children down for takeoff, Mike cautiously gravitated toward Zoe. Her waist-length hair had been confined into a single plait snaking down her back, although a few shorter strands dangled in front of her triple-studded ears. She'd pushed up the sleeves of her bulky persimmon-colored sweater, the color phenomenally striking against her golden skin and black hair, all of her striking against the muted beiges and grays and granites of the plane's interior. She sat with one tan-legginged leg tucked up under her, her ankle-high tan lace-up shoes discarded at her feet. Her socks, he noticed with a smile, had jack-o'-lanterns all over them.

She was frowning, the expression bracketing her full mouth with tiny lines he found he wanted to soothe away. Any way he could. *Kissing* sprang to mind as a good choice.

He caught his breath, plastered on a smile he hoped didn't look as goony as it felt.

"Hi, there."

He sensed her hesitation before looking up at him, as if weighing the significance of the gesture.

"Oh. Hello."

That was it.

"May...I join you?" He indicated the high-backed seat next to hers.

"Up to you," she said, her attention back on her work.

He'd missed her. How he could miss someone he barely knew was a mystery he decided he'd rather not unravel. And how he could miss someone whose presence was, half the time, about as pleasant as itching powder, was even more beyond his comprehension. But he had. Avoiding her had done nothing to quiet either the attraction or the longing. Nor had constant reminders of his erratic life-style. Even though he knew it was probably wrong and pointless and would undoubtedly lead to frustration and a helluva lot of sleepless nights, he still wanted to dig underneath the wall Zoe Chan had built around her heart, and find out who she really was.

He'd just have to figure out the rest of it later.

But first he had to get her to talk to him. He reached over and touched her wrist. She jumped a foot.

"Is something the matter?" he asked.

Her eyes were nearly opaque, like dusty coal, as if she couldn't focus clearly. "Why on earth would anything be the matter?"

"You're not exactly giving me a warm welcome."

Now the eyes narrowed. "Oh, gee—sorry. The trumpeters and flower girls have the night off. I'm busy, Mr. Kwan. That's all. If you want to sit here, fine. It's not as if I'm saving the seat for anyone else. But I'm in the middle of something I'd like to get done before we get to New York, so I'm afraid I won't be very good company." Then she went back to her work.

Something was definitely screwy here. She couldn't possibly know what she'd agreed to. Besides that, they had left each other on good terms, three weeks before. Why was she acting like this?

What had he done, agreeing to "meet" her? He'd figured he was safe, playing along with her sister. Judging from Zoe's comments about her family's matchmaking attempts, he'd thought surely she'd point-blank refuse. But she hadn't. Why? Why had she agreed to meet someone she already knew? And why wasn't she saying anything? Was she playing some sort of game?

Or could it be that she really didn't know?

His guess would have been that she would have been furious, or amused, or maybe even disgusted, but it was a pretty safe bet she would have been *something*. He doubted whether Zoe had ever been neutral about anything in her life. So how on earth had Margi managed to pull this off?

And what, if anything, was he going to do about it?

He finally lowered his briefcase to the floor beside the seat, removed his suit jacket and sat down.

She continued to ignore him. So he waved in front of her face.

"Go away."

"I thought you said I could sit here?"

Her eyes flitted up to his face, then back to the computer. "I thought you agreed to leave me alone?"

"I never agreed to that. You assumed I would honor your request."

Her sigh was impossible to misconstrue. "You are so full of it, you know that?" she muttered.

Hmm. They were back to that, were they? "Is that what you really think?"

That stopped her, for a moment. During this entire exchange, she hadn't stopped once, her small hands seeming to operate independently of her head and her mouth. "Mr. Kwan," she said quietly, "you don't want to know what I really think."

Something in her voice clutched at his chest, but he forced himself not to react. Instead, he crossed his ankle over his knee, then leaned his chin in his palm and stared at her as she worked. Fascinated. And determined to get her goat. After a moment or two, the tactic worked.

"*What?*" Now her eyes glittered like faceted jet; he speared them with his and wouldn't let go.

"I'm just trying to figure out why you think I'm one step up from toxic waste."

Her delicate brows lifted, just slightly, underneath those wispy bangs. But she didn't look away. "Who said anything about a step *up?*"

"Ohhh—low blow. But you know—last time I checked, I didn't kick kittens or cheat little old ladies out of their life savings. In fact, some people even think I'm a nice guy—"

"See?" she interrupted. "*Nice* guys don't have to go around *telling* people they're nice guys—"

A flight attendant came by, asked them what they'd like to drink, and reminded them to fasten their seat belts for the imminent takeoff.

"Good point," Mike belatedly replied, clicking his belt into place. "So give me a chance to prove it. Have dinner with me tomorrow night."

He hadn't expected her to laugh.

"You are truly amazing, you know that? Why would I do that? Have I given you one single, solitary clue that I would be in the least bit amenable to going out with you?"

"I took the fact that you didn't throw the laptop at me as a positive sign."

She laughed again. "Brother, you do grasp at straws, don't you?"

"I'm a salesman," he said with a grin. "What can I tell you?"

"Very little. Trust me," she shot back. "And I wouldn't get my hopes up if I were you. Not even *you're* worth destroying a three-thousand-dollar computer for."

"Oh…" He put his hand over his heart. "Now I *am* hurt." Leaning forward, he gently cuffed her wrist. "But I still want to have dinner with you."

She jerked her hand away, then immediately looked as

though she regretted the move. And with that move he understood. Not about Margi's arrangement—that was still a mystery. But what Zoe was doing.

She was running scared—he was sure of it. Afraid of him, or at least of getting involved.

And how could he blame her?

"Remember?" she said, returning her attention to the computer. "I don't eat dinner."

Don't do this, warned a voice in his head. *Leave it be.*

"Ever?"

"Not with men."

You're a fool, Kwan.

"We've already had lunch—"

"That was different."

"Zoe, look at me."

All she offered was a sideways glance. But it was enough. Enough to know he was probably about to make a mistake. Enough to know that he had no choice. Except to go slowly.

"I have no hidden agenda. I'm not going to try to get you into my hotel room, or ply you with insincere sweet talk. I like you, okay? That's it. And I'd like to share a meal with you. Period. Can you deal with that?"

Before she could answer, the engines revved to begin the taxi to the runway. But he could have sworn he saw something resembling disappointment in her eyes.

7

The roar of the engines pretty much matched the roar in her head. He *liked* her. That's what he said, anyway. Did she dare believe him? Did she dare trust a man whose lifework was convincing people to buy things they didn't really need?

Did she dare trust herself?

And…was this a step in the right direction, or the end of the road?

One thing she *didn't* dare do was tell him she felt the same way. Because, for one thing, it still didn't make sense. The man still irritated the life out of her. Sometimes. But she had to admit he was smart. Funny. Savvy.

And sexy. But she didn't want to go *there*, because she'd been *there* before. And *there* was bad news.

For the past twenty-four hours she'd tried to imagine how she'd feel, how'd she react, when she saw him again. Nothing had prepared her for the reality. Stress indicators? She had 'em all. Sweaty palms. Shortness of breath. A stomach that felt like a trampoline with a dozen little kids jumping on it—while wearing soccer cleats.

But the reaction that most freaked her was the inexplicable desire to know how that finely shaped mouth kissed. What it would feel like to be held in his arms. To touch his hair, his face, his chest. To *be* touched.

And maybe, someday, to be loved. To be loved by someone as honest and intelligent and forthright and generous as the man who had just asked her to dinner tomorrow night.

But all she was being given right now was *like*.

"*Hey—it's a start,*" whispered the little creature living under her rib cage.

She leaned her head back against the seat and shut her eyes, considering the novelty of this arrangement. *If* she could believe him, *if* she could trust him, well...

Well.

As the plane lifted off, Brianna's one-year-old started to cry with the abrupt pressure change; seconds later, Zoe could hear Spencer soothing the little boy.

Grateful for the diversion, she opened her eyes and studied the prematurely silver-haired man she'd thought so arrogant when she first met him three years ago, a man who turned out to have the class and courage and conviction of his feelings to marry a woman pregnant with another man's child. A man that Brianna couldn't speak of, even in an off-handed way, without her features softening into an expression Zoe was sure she'd never experienced. Had thought, before tonight, that she never would.

The plane leveled out; the flight attendant brought them their drinks, a ginger ale for her, a Coke for Mike. As Zoe sipped her drink, she watched Spencer unhook the still-sobbing Tyler from his seat belt and take the baby into his lap. The child went immediately quiet, rubbing his nose into Spencer's cotton sweater, then sticking his thumb into his mouth. And Zoe saw the look of contentment that passed between Brianna and Spencer. Spencer winked and grinned at his wife, who then settled the almost-three-year-old Melissa onto her lap and began to softly read to her from a dog-eared copy of *The Cat in the Hat*.

Zoe's breath caught in her throat at the sweetness of the scene. But she was no fool. Brianna and Spencer's union was no less subject to the pitfalls common to the institution than anyone else's. Spencer's needing to be away so much—often unexpectedly, which threw off Brianna's plans—was a constant challenge for both of them. And she knew that Tyler had tantrums that tried his parents' patience, that it had taken forever to get Melissa potty-trained, that Brianna had been beside herself when her daughter had ''painted'' the white leather sofa in their library with lipstick or led a horde of muddy-footed mites across the freshly cleaned living room carpet.

Despite the couple's wealth and success and advantages, it still wasn't easy. But nothing was going to mess with the glue of respect and loyalty and unconditional love that held that relationship together. When Spencer and Brianna looked at each other, they saw nothing else.

That, Zoe realized, was what she wanted. And nothing less.

She felt as if her brain was cramping from trying to think so hard. Even a simple dinner date could be dangerous, if she wasn't careful. Mike would have to go some to win her heart, and, at the moment, that didn't seem to be his goal. And he'd been right about how much a career could interfere with a relationship. She saw the toll it was taking on her sister, how edgy Spencer's frequent absences made Brianna. Would Zoe be happy being a part-time wife, sharing her husband, that much, with his business?

She was scared, she realized. To death. It was one thing to get hurt by someone who turned out to be a jerk anyway. Putting yourself in the position to be hurt by someone *good*... She frowned, having no idea how to complete her thought.

But what the hell. It was just dinner, right?

''Mike?''

He slanted his head toward her, his brows lifted.

If all he could offer was friendship, perhaps she could live with that. After all, it wasn't as if they were exactly beating down her door. One step at a time, she told herself.

''Where did you have in mind for dinner?'' she asked, completely unprepared for her heart's *sproinnnng* when he smiled for her.

And the little voice said, *''Good girl.''*

There was no arguing with the Lockharts, Mike quickly discovered. First, it was the plane. Then, a lift in the limo to his hotel. Which quickly became an invitation to stay at their

Fifth Avenue penthouse as their guest. Not having been raised by raccoons in the woods, he politely demurred, knowing they would insist a second time, at which point he could accept with a clear conscience. Which, indeed, was exactly what had happened.

And if Zoe had been a bit more enthusiastic about the arrangement, he might have been, as well.

She'd been fine, chatty even, until Brianna issued the invitation. Then, *wham!* The door slammed shut—again—and it was "So-sorry-but-we're-closed-for-the-day."

They spoke little the rest of the plane trip, each one immersed in his or her work. He found himself concerned, though, at how often he caught Zoe rubbing her eyes or the back of her neck. Having experienced the symptoms himself, all too often, he well knew the signs of overwork. Now, in the limo on the way to the Lockharts' Fifth Avenue apartment, she had melted against the leather seat next to him, her head lying heavily in her hand as she gazed out the window. Had they been alone, he might have been tempted to gather her against his chest and lull her to sleep, like he might a child.

It was a good thing for him, then, that they weren't alone.

Spencer, Brianna and the two zonked-out toddlers sat opposite them in the forward-facing seat. Brianna, too, seemed either preoccupied or exhausted, quietly stroking her son's cornsilk waves as he snoozed on her lap. Which left Spencer as the only one to talk to on the half-hour drive into Manhattan from La Guardia.

Mike found himself surprisingly impressed with the soft-spoken Lockhart, who, in turn, seemed not at all impressed by either his position or the money that had put him there. He was, however, extremely proud of his business, talking about it with the same fondness—and intensity—as he did his children. Mike knew from keeping his ear to the ground that Spencer had inherited the huge personal-products conglomerate from his father, now deceased more than eight years. On the flight up, Zoe had further explained how the unlikely tycoon had nurtured his father's legacy in order for it to grow even more. In doing so, Mike realized, the man was providing literally thousands of solid jobs utilizing a broad spectrum of skills. Spencer Lockhart was wealthy, yes. But not at anyone else's expense, as far as Mike could tell.

In turn, Spencer listened attentively to Mike as he spoke of his little agency, his plans for it and for the people who trusted him to market their products and services.

"Your business means a great deal to you," Spencer said softly so as not to wake the children. It wasn't a question.

"Yes," Mike replied, equally direct.

Spencer nodded, then asked, "How many hours a day do you put in?"

"It varies. Never less than ten. As many as sixteen if I'm backed against a wall."

Another nod, then a trenchant regard. "I used to do that, too," he said mildly. His gaze drifted to his dozing wife, then back to Mike. Even in the half-light inside the limo, the man's eyes were the sharpest, clearest blue Mike had ever seen. "Until I discovered I didn't need to."

Before Mike could think of a reply, the limo pulled up in front of the apartment building. As the Lockharts gathered up assorted sleeping toddlers and left the car, Mike glanced over at Zoe.

She, too, was sound asleep. He reached over, slowly drawing one knuckle down a whisper-soft cheek. His breath caught in his throat at his body's reaction. After years of living with an easily subdued sex drive, now, with just one touch, his hormones came roaring out of nowhere like a million football players barreling toward the same goal line.

He drew back his hand as she awakened, her sooty lashes fluttering for a second before popping open.

"Oh!" she said, then yawned. "Are we here?"

Mike smiled at her, loving how her brow knotted at the slightest provocation. "Since Brianna and Spencer just got out with the kids, I assume so."

There was no answer, just another yawn, as she gathered up her tote bag and laptop. Then, suddenly, she looked at him, her eyes soft-focused and sleepy and questioning. Her hand drifted up to her cheek, her own fingers following the trail his had just left.

"Did you—?"

The limo door opened on her side, and a booming voice welcomed her back to New York.

The spell was broken. Mike saw her shake her head, catch her breath, then swing her legs out to the sidewalk.

"Thanks, Enrique," she said, letting the doorman assist her out of the limo. "It's good to be back."

It was unusually warm for October. Especially at 2:00 a.m.

Seated in the black cast-iron chair on the penthouse's terrace, wearing only her satin pajamas and robe, Zoe wasn't even shivering. It was almost hauntingly quiet this time of night, the traffic noise twenty stories below muted and sporadic. She hadn't even heard a siren in the last half hour.

No surprise that she was awake. Since college, she had learned to make the most of a catnap, and a fifteen-minute snooze could keep her going for another four or five hours.

Even so, these middle-of-the-night wanderings had become a regular occurrence these past few weeks. Exhausted from overwork, she'd collapse into a dead sleep at eleven, only to awaken a few hours later, wired and unable to get back to sleep. And always, with the wakefulness came an unsettling sense of something being wrong, out of sync, out of focus. Then, come morning, exhausted and even more irritable, she'd throw herself back into her job, hoping the occupation would keep the willies at bay, make her too tired to dream, to waken.

Only, every night, the cycle would begin again. Tonight, however, there was something more specific to unsettle her: Michael Kwan. Even more specifically, Michael Kwan's unexpected proximity.

He'd touched her, in the limo while she was still asleep. She was sure of it. She wasn't sure what upset her more—that he'd touched her, or that she'd missed it.

Damn Spencer and Brianna and their Southern hospitality.

Here she'd finally gotten up the nerve to have dinner with the man, and they up and invite him to spend nearly a week!

This week, she thought with a groan. She laid her head back, closing her eyes. Not a comforting thought. Before, when they'd come up for Market, she and Brianna would go to the other vendors' shows, write their orders, and that was it. This time, because Brianna would be tied up showing her own line, Zoe would have to attend all the buying appointments on her own, as well as help set up for the show and mop up afterward. Even though they had hired a couple of temps with Seventh Avenue experience to help with the shows and buying appointments, any way she looked at it, the majority of the work was about to land in her lap. Again.

Her eyes still closed, she frowned, mentally squinting, as if trying to focus on something in the distance. Was it the workload itself that was bothering her, she wondered, or the fact that, if she didn't have the work, there'd be nothing else?

"Figures," she heard behind her, "if I came out here at 2:00 a.m. to be alone, you'd already be here."

By rights, she should have jumped out of her skin. That she didn't startled her even more than his sudden appearance.

Sensing that Mike was the type who loved to ferret out people's troubles, she forced herself to look relaxed, propping her feet up on the matching iron table in front of her. All her life, Zoe had worked out her own problems. She'd never felt her business was anyone else's. And she wasn't about to change that policy now. Even if she didn't know what the problem was that had to be worked out. All she knew was that she didn't want Mike to become one of the problems.

Oh, yeah. That much she knew. And at 2:00 a.m., you take what you can get.

"Bet it'll be cold in the morning," he volunteered.

She twisted herself to look at him. Or where she supposed he was. With no moon, the darkness bordered on opaque. A sliver of light from the open French doors behind him only haloed his silhouette; she couldn't see his face at all. She thought maybe he was standing with his hands in his pockets. Which meant he was still dressed. At this hour?

Like it was any of her business, right?

"What makes you think that?"

His shoes softly crunched against the brick terrace floor as he crossed to the stone railing, surveyed the city below. "Those clouds over there." He nodded to his right. "The ring around the moon earlier, before it set. A certain…feel to the air." He turned. She could sense the grin she couldn't see. "And I listened to the eleven o'clock news. Weatherman said the temperature was going to drop by dawn."

She shook her head, smiling in spite of herself. "Are you always this perverse?"

"Every chance I get." She could tell he'd crossed his arms over his chest as he leaned his hips against the railing.

Her elbows balanced on the arms of the chair, she bridged her loosely clasped hands over her stomach. "This could be dangerous."

"Oh?" He moved closer, sat down in the chair beside hers, the iron scraping for a second against the bricks.

"Yeah. I mean, this might mean we have something in common. Discovering our mutual nocturnal tendencies."

Her peripheral vision caught a glint from what she supposed was a smile. "And why is that dangerous?"

"It just is."

"Is this supposed to be female logic?"

"Is that supposed to be a comment from an enlightened male?"

"If I was enlightened, I would have understood what you just said."

She cocked her head at him. "Well, I have to give you one thing. You may be perverse, but you're not a fool."

Mike smiled again, then leaned back in his chair, assuming a pose identical to hers. "So…why are you awake?"

"Because I'm not asleep," she shot back, only to be rewarded with a gentle laugh.

"Yeah. Overwork makes me tighter than a coiled spring, too."

Something snapped in the back of her brain. "What makes you think I'm overworked—?"

"Zoe, please." He reached over and insinuated his warm, smooth fingers around hers. To her surprise, she let them stay. "I know the signs, remember? Not to mention every time I've been in to see you and Brianna, you're trying to juggle a hundred balls at once." He paused, gently squeezed her hand. "And I bet you haven't said one word to her, have you?"

"You're imagining things."

"Am I?"

Unexplainably irritated, she stood, stuffing her hands into her pockets. "Well. On second thought, I'm suddenly sleepy. I'll see you in the—"

He had stood, as well. "Why are you mad at me, Zoe?"

She liked the way he said her name, softening the *e* on the end into a gentle "eh" sound, rather than the harsher "ee" most people used. "I'm not mad at you or anyone else," she said, starting back inside.

But he caught her before her hand reached the doorknob, twirled her around and enclosed her in his arms.

Not to kiss her, she realized after a moment's panic. Just to hold her.

For some reason, that was even worse. A kiss would have been a pass, which would have given her cause to slug him, maybe. At least let out an indignant gasp and storm back into the apartment.

This was...not a pass. She didn't think, anyway. Still, she was sure he could feel her heart pounding in her own chest as he held her close, one hand calmly stroking her head.

He smelled of fireplace smoke, from the fire that had been waiting for them when they'd arrived earlier, traces of end-of-the-day after-shave, and something else that was just *him*. It was nice. Too nice probably.

For a moment, she felt as safe as a child, in her father's arms. But something else, decidedly not safe, curled inside her belly, electrifying and quickening and frightening her. With a sharp intake of breath, she pulled back.

One strong, firm hand still on her arm, Mike said gently, "It's just a hug, honey. That's all." His other hand reached up to her face, searing her cheek where his fingers traced a delicate path on her skin. "When was the last time you had a hug?"

There was just enough light to see his face, to see the contradiction in his features. The creased brow, the steady, unblinking eyes, the mouth flirting with the idea of a smile.

With a sigh, she settled against his chest. Safe. Protected. And, whether she liked it or not, or wanted it or not, a little bit in love.

Through a constricted throat, she tried to joke. "My mother, on Sunday."

He laughed, dropping a quick kiss on the top of her head. "Mothers don't count. Now *they* have hidden agendas."

"And you don't?"

He suddenly steered her toward the door, draping one arm loosely over her shoulders. Deliberately not answering her question. "Think they've got any hot chocolate in this joint?" he asked with a good-natured grin as he guided her back into the apartment.

Once inside, she twisted to face him, throwing him slightly off-balance. She'd hoped the stronger light would reveal more of what was going on in his head, would give her a clue as to what he really wanted from her. It didn't.

And she was too tired, too confused and too scared to ask. Because, no matter what his answer might be, she wasn't sure what she'd do with the information.

So. One small curiosity satisfied. She felt good in his arms. Terrifyingly good.

And right.

Mike stretched out in bed, one arm braced behind his head, staring into darkness so black, he could practically feel it.

Zoe had hit the nail on the head when she'd called him

perverse. But she'd been dead wrong about his not being a
fool. Only someone this perverse—and this much of a fool—
would be lying here at three in the morning wondering how
to go about pursuing a woman who *a)* probably didn't even
like him very much and *b)* he wasn't sure he'd know what to
do with even if he did get something going with her.

He wouldn't go so far as to call this whatever-it-was burn-
ing inside him *love.* But it wasn't *lust,* either. Not really. Oh,
yeah, he was sure his body temperature went up a couple of
degrees whenever he was around her, and she'd worked her
way into a couple of interesting dreams in the past few weeks.
But lust wasn't known for its patience. And he was willing to
be patient. He thought anyway, remembering the helmeted
hormones from earlier in the evening.

He flopped over in the bed, scrunching the pillow under his
head. Closed his eyes. Realized he could smell her perfume—
faintly—on his hand.

For both their sakes, he would be patient.

The hot chocolate had worked like a charm. She'd been
asleep within seconds of turning out her light. Now, somewhat
awake and dressed at seven-fifteen the next morning, Zoe
sipped Colombian coffee at the wrought-iron-and-marble table
set in a bay window on one side of the penthouse's overlarge
kitchen. Across the table sat an adorable three-year-old girl
well versed in the age-old art of little-finger-wrapping, her
quarry being Colleen O'Hara, the penthouse's housekeeper.

The sixtyish woman was in heaven with her little charges.
Brianna had mentioned bringing the children's nanny up with
them, but Colleen had taken such offense that Brianna had
immediately changed her plans. After twenty-some years of
nothing more than keeping the apartment ready for Spencer's
occasional visits and the odd meal here and there, the chance
to care for two precocious, adorable kids was better than winning the lottery, far as Colleen was concerned.

Zoe sighed, somewhat contented, tucking one arm against
her ribs. Judging from the antique radiators' clanks and hisses,

it had indeed turned sharply colder overnight. The kitchen smelled *good*—freshly brewed coffee and steam heat and that rich, aged aroma of a well-cared-for Pre-War apartment. The room was quintessentially New York, a hodgepodge of old and new, with its chessboard tile floor and state-of-the-art Euro-style appliances, the glass-paned cupboards sporting a dozen coats of white enamel paint set on walls thickly troweled to hide the imperfections from decades of settling. In the three years since Brianna's marriage, Zoe had been here perhaps a half-dozen times. It never ceased to amaze her how homey and *real* a place it was, its size and opulence notwithstanding.

"Where's Mommy?" Melissa asked, fisting her Cheerios into her mouth.

"Now, you just let your mother be, angel," Colleen said with a wink at Zoe and an accent straight out of an old Barry Fitzgerald movie. "Mom and Dad need their sleep, they do." She turned back to the batter she was making for French toast, but said over her shoulder, "So tell me about the handsome man asleep in the other guest room."

Zoe put down her coffee mug a little harder than she intended to. "You had already gone to bed when we got in, Colleen. How do you know who—or even *what*, for that matter—is in there?"

"Little pitchers have even bigger mouths than ears," Colleen said with a nod toward the curly-headed imp tilting her empty bowl up to drain all the milk from it. "Said he was handsome, she did. Tall, but not as tall as her daddy. And had black hair and eyes, just like yours."

Zoe sank her cheek in her hand, regarding the miniature Brianna on the other side of the table. "Well, did she happen to have access to his credit rating, too?"

"Give her a minute," Colleen said with a chuckle, "and I'm sure she'll get around to it, the lamb."

With renewed respect, Zoe eyed "the lamb," her perusal interrupted when Brianna swept into the kitchen, her shoulder-length hair in disarray, an ivory satin robe haphazardly sashed around her slender waist.

"Good morning, Colleen!" she said with a bright smile, bussing the housekeeper on the cheek. "Hi, sweetie." She greeted her daughter with another kiss and an all-out hug, then said to Colleen, "Do we still have one of those insulated mugs around that Spencer could take some coffee in? We must have overslept—"

As she chattered, she opened and closed cupboards, the robe slipping open enough to reveal the absence of a nightgown underneath. Colleen tossed Zoe a wink, then ambled over to the one cupboard Brianna had missed, pulling out the mug. She rinsed it out, filled it with coffee, then handed it back to Brianna, who offered a breathless "Thanks" and flew back out of the room.

Colleen burst out laughing.

"What's so funny?" Melissa asked.

"Oh, nothing, sweet angel," Colleen said, collecting the empty cereal bowl and dumping it into a basin of sudsy water. As she washed it, she said, "Don't think I've ever seen two people more in love than those two. Or who deserve it more. Well," she said, placing the clean bowl in the drainer, then drying her hands on her apron, "I best be getting your little brother out of bed, don't you think?" She held out one plump hand to the little girl. "Come with me, lamb?"

With an eager nod, the child wriggled down off her chair and hopped over to the housekeeper, her hand outstretched. After Colleen and Melissa headed out the kitchen's back door, Zoe got up and wandered into the dining room with her coffee. Bright indirect light filtered in through a bank of west-facing windows overlooking Central Park. The cold front had left the air clear enough to almost make out details in buildings miles away in New Jersey on the east bank of the Hudson. Central Park below was a kaleidoscope of russets and golds and crimsons of the changing trees, underneath a cloudless sky so vibrant Zoe felt as if she could reach out and touch it.

She heard voices at the front door which, despite the length of the rooms between here and there, she could see from where she stood.

It was highly unlikely, however, that Brianna and Spencer would notice her.

He was dressed for the breakfast appointment Zoe knew he had, traffic-stopping handsome in his charcoal suit and black cashmere topcoat, his attaché case clasped in his left hand. Brianna, however, was still in her robe, although she'd brushed her hair, which now glistened from the skylight over the center of the vestibule. Zoe couldn't hear what they were saying, but whatever the conversation, it was freely punctuated with laughter. Private, intimate laughter, low and soft.

Finally, Spencer put his hand on the doorknob to leave, prompting Brianna to tilt her face up to his for a goodbye kiss. Spencer accepted the docile peck on the lips, grinned, then released the doorknob and slid his free hand around to the small of Brianna's back, pulling their pelvises together. With another, throatier, laugh, Brianna looped her hands around her husband's neck and melted into a kiss that was anything but docile this time.

Suddenly aware that she had become an unwitting voyeur, Zoe stepped back into the room, turned around.

And ran smack into Mike Kwan's steady gaze not ten feet away.

8

Like a blast of summer heat when you walk out of an overly air-conditioned building, the realization slapped her that only once before had she seen him in anything other than a business suit, or at least a dress shirt and tie. The graceful, if somewhat untidy, collection of long, lean muscles softly sheathed in navy silk pajama bottoms and a casually open robe set her pulse rate bopping.

If he'd been wearing *that* when he'd hugged her the night before…

"Oh" was all she could manage, her brain having ceased all reliable function.

He lifted his coffee cup to her, a wide grin bisecting his morning-roughened features. "Morning." The gesture parted the robe even more, giving her an unobstructed view of most of his chest. And there was a lot to view.

This morning, it seemed that everywhere she looked, she shouldn't.

"Have you had breakfast yet?" he asked, shoving his heavy hair off his forehead, only to have it fall right back the instant he removed his hand.

She shook her head.

He backed up, pushed open the swinging door. "Then come on *in*," he said in an exaggerated drawl, "and let's see what all we can rustle up."

"If that's supposed to be a country accent," she said, walking past him through the door, "it's terrible."

"I know. That's why I did it. Just to yank your chain."

She glanced back, fully prepared to glower at him. One look at that mischievous face, however, and all she could do was laugh.

The kitchen had been empty when he'd strayed in via the back entrance a minute or so earlier. After pouring himself a cup of coffee, he decided to take a tour of the magnificent apartment, starting with the dining room.

Zoe apparently hadn't heard the swinging door when he pushed it open, hadn't noticed when he entered the room. At first, she'd been staring out the window, the stark light from the curtainless windows limning her flawless profile. She'd pulled her slippery hair back with a silver banana comb so that it fell in lazy waves past the middle of her back. She reminded him of some sort of exotic bird in her silky royal blue tunic and matching leggings, over which she wore the beaded and jeweled vest he remembered from before. Tiny feet, delicate feet, were encased in suede flats the same blue as her outfit.

When she suddenly gravitated toward the door between the dining room and living room, curiosity enticed him to take a step—or two—closer to see what had caught her attention. Then he, too, caught a glimpse of Brianna and Spencer at the door, clearly the picture of two people who, he'd wager, had made love within the past hour.

Blatantly he watched Zoe watching them. And wondered what she was thinking.

When she'd turned to him, for just an instant he thought maybe he knew. But whatever he'd thought he'd seen flitted over her features like a wispy cloud, too insubstantial to even cast a shadow in passing. She hadn't, however, been able to control her blush.

Now, smooth and cool as polished lapis, she sat on a stool alongside one of the granite-topped counters, hugging her mug of coffee to her chest as if it was telling her secrets. Starved by this point, Mike began to forage, crossing the front flaps of his robe over his chest and yanking tight the sash. Over the coffee aroma, he could smell her perfume.

This wasn't going to be easy.

"When did you get up?" he heard behind him.

"Seven," he said, finally taking a sip of the coffee he'd been carrying around with him for ten minutes, which had gone lukewarm in the interim. "I have a nine o'clock meeting in Brooklyn. A new client."

"What is it this time?" When he looked at her, she was smiling. *That* he liked. Which was more than he could say for the circles under her eyes.

"Tennis balls, believe it or not."

She leaned one elbow back on the counter and tilted her head at him. A stray sunbeam caressed the sweep of her hair tumbling over one shoulder. His fingers tingled. "How, may I ask, does one market tennis balls?" she asked, then lifted the mug to her lips.

"Aggressively."

She chuckled into her coffee.

"Do you know what sort of batter this is?" he asked, lifting the bowl of eggy-looking stuff off the stove.

"French toast." Zoe put her coffee on the counter, then pulled one foot up onto the top rung of the stool, linking her fingers around her knee. "Colleen's on baby duty this morning, so she'll be back soon. Hope you don't mind breakfast with small children around."

Mike snorted, then started looking for some bread, which he found in an old-fashioned roll-up bin on top of one of the other counters. "When it comes to food, I could eat in the middle of a nuclear holocaust. Besides, I think those are two of the cutest kids since Spanky and Our Gang. This the bread she was going to use?" He held up the Pepperidge Farm package.

Zoe shrugged. "Sorry. Can't help you there. So...you like kids?"

Ah. There *was* a woman under there. "Not all, and not all the time. But I love my cousins' kids. And those two." Then he turned the heat on underneath the griddle and he saw her foot drop.

"What are you doing?" He thought he detected a touch of horror in her voice.

"Making breakfast. What else?"

"I don't think Colleen's going to like this—"

He soaked a piece of bread in the egg mixture, tossed it onto the hot griddle. Then another. "How many pieces would you like?"

"Oh…uh, two, I guess. Did you hear what I said?"

"Yeah. Is there syrup around?"

"I have no idea—Mike!"

He calmly added two more slices before acknowledging her. "Yeah?"

"She's gonna kill you!"

"Then at least I'll go on a full stomach." He flipped the pieces already on the grill. "See if you can find the syrup, would you?"

After a moment of apparent incredulity, Zoe slid off the stool and began rummaging in the cupboards, then in the refrigerator, until she found an assortment of syrups, each and every one mouthwateringly expensive.

"Is that really blackberry?" he asked, nodding in the direction of one she showed him.

"That okay?"

He laughed. "I was thinking along the lines of Log Cabin. Yeah, I think I could live with blackberry."

Then, in a flurry of Irish brogue and high-pitched baby talk, the legendary Colleen returned. Melissa skipped ahead and climbed back into her booster chair at the table, patting Tyler's high chair and calling to him to join her. The baby, however, complete with sleep-tousled curls and "blankie" imprints on his soft cheeks, was happily ensconced on Colleen's formidable hip, his thumb securely in his mouth as his wheat-lashed cobalt blue eyes took in the room.

When Colleen spotted Mike, she froze, inexplicably switching the baby to her other hip. As if performing some primitive dance, Mike in turn shifted the spatula to his left hand, then held out his right, realizing as he did at least six feet separated them.

"Good morning, Mrs. O'Hara. Hope you don't mind that I got things started." He smiled. "Especially as you had enough to do with the children."

"I tried to warn him, Colleen," Zoe began, but Colleen's swipe at the air vaguely in Zoe's direction stopped her short.

"You know how to cook?" she asked, squinting at him.

"Purely a survival instinct," he said, neatly turning the pieces of toast out onto a warm plate. "I love to eat. But I don't love to eat junk. So I learned to cook. French cuisine is my specialty, with Italian following a close second."

Out of the corner of his eye, he caught Zoe's eyebrows rise. Her eyes still narrowed, Colleen approached the stove, critically eyeing the finished product. "That'll do well enough, I guess," she said after a moment. "Just don't you be makin' a mess and then not cleanin' it up, young man."

"Not to worry, Mrs. O'Hara," he said. "A gentleman never leaves messes for a lady to clean up."

"Ha!" the older woman replied, clearly unconvinced, then addressed Zoe. "Did Spencer leave, then?" she asked as she slid Tyler into his high chair.

Mike felt a prickle of awareness—okay, arousal—when Zoe glanced at him before responding. Neither had said a word about witnessing the passionate goodbye a few minutes before. He doubted either of them would. But, for whatever it might or might not be worth, they had shared it. It was difficult to watch two people that much in love—and that demonstrative—and not at least give a passing thought to one's own lack in that department. At least, that had been Mike's reaction. Had Zoe felt that, too?

"Yes," she said, her fingers now worrying the beads on her vest. "A few minutes ago." She flicked him the briefest of glances, then blushed again.

Yeah. She'd felt it. If he was clever, he could use that to his advantage. He wasn't sure how yet, or when he should.

But it was there. Like one of the extra guys in those video games his cousins played that you can exchange for another turn when your regular allotment of guys runs out.

"That'll be Brianna's shower water I hear runnin', then, so she'll not be in to breakfast for a while." Colleen picked up the plate Mike had fixed for Zoe, and his as well, from the side of the stove and carried it toward the dining room. "You two better eat in here," she said, backing her way into the room through the swinging door. "Otherwise, you're liable to get oatmeal splattered all over you, if Tyler's table manners are anything like his sister's were at that age. Well, just don't stand there—get out here while you have a chance!"

They obeyed, carrying their coffee and juice out to the cherrywood table already set with Madeira linens, sterling flatwear, Baccarat crystal.

Something had happened. The smiling, teasing young woman in the kitchen had vanished, replaced by...whoever this was across from him. They sat in awkward silence for several minutes, like strangers forced to sit together in a crowded restaurant. Mike noticed that Zoe was only picking at her breakfast rather than eating it.

"You don't like it?"

His sudden comment made her jump, nearly losing her fork. After a second or two of fumbling with it, she brought it under control. Sort of. Her hand trembled, and he had the distinct feeling she was fighting tears.

He covered her hand with his own. "Zoe—hey...what's the matter?"

She snatched her hand away as if he'd reprimanded her. "Nothing," she snapped, then took a deep breath. "Nothing. Really. I'm just...tired, that's all. I don't travel very well, and it throws off my whole system for a day or two. I'm fine, though."

He resumed eating, forcing himself to stop scrutinizing her. She was lying. Of that much he was certain. Her comment about not traveling well was not lost on him, however. And he was pretty sure she wasn't lying about that. And since he traveled so much...

"So...what are your plans for the day?" he asked. Cautiously.

"Whatever Brianna needs me to do," she said, torturing a piece of French toast with the tines of her fork. "Begin steaming out the gowns, make final arrangements for the show setup. Whatever."

He put a bite of the toast into his mouth, chewed for a second. After a sip of juice, he said quietly, "And what would you rather be doing?"

Her eyes—startled and, he thought, more than a little fearful—shot to his face. Then he saw her visibly rein in her emotions. She looked away. "I'm not here on my time," she said. "This is a business trip, not a vacation."

"And you never combine the two?"

"Brianna's not paying me to play, Mike."

Now he leaned forward, lowering his voice. "And you expect me to believe that your employer *doesn't?*"

"She works incredibly hard—"

"I'm sure she does. And I'm duly impressed. But her assistant's getting run into the ground. How many weekends do you get off?"

Her laugh was more like a sharp bark. "I'm in the *wedding* business, for heaven's sake! Working on weekends comes with the territory. Besides—how many do *you?* Who's got a business meeting in an hour? What is this—some chauvinistic double standard? It's okay for the man to work whenever he needs to, but not the woman? When it's your own business, you don't get weekends. You said so yourself. That's why you can't have a relationship. Isn't that what you said?"

An amazing thing, this way women had of cramming a half-dozen subjects into one dialogue exchange. Yes, they were discussing working on weekends. But years of salesmanship had taught him to tune in to the other stations in the area. He heard annoyance at his supposed double standard, a probably unrecognized resentment at having to work so hard, and an unmistakable sting—also probably unrecognized—about his not being able to have a relationship.

Or maybe that part was wishful thinking.

He decided to tackle the surface problem, the first one. The second would probably lead directly into a can of worms he wasn't ready to deal with, and the third—oh, Lord. He didn't know *what* to do about the third. Especially not at seven-thirty in the morning. "But this isn't your business, Zoe," he ventured. "It's Brianna's. And she's got her husband and kids here with her, so she's at least trying to maintain her personal life, as well. What are you getting out of this?"

"This is my life, Mike," Zoe said, staring hard at her plate. Then, suddenly, she pinned him with her gaze. While there were no tears evident, if she thought she was masking how upset she was, she was sadly mistaken. "Okay. Since you're hell-bent on making a mountain out of a molehill, let me set you straight. I've been working for and with Brianna for four years. She's been wonderful to me. I've learned more from her about marketing and sales and the nuts and bolts of running a business than I did in all my business degree coursework put together. She pays extremely well, she never quibbles about my taking personal time and she's always treated me as an equal, despite my being so much younger than she. I owe her a great deal, not the least of which is my loyalty. Look—things have just been nuts these past several weeks, so I've been working more than usual. But once we get the line up and running, things should calm down."

"And this is what you want? To work yourself into the ground for something that's not even yours?"

After a long moment, she said, "Sometimes, what we want has nothing to do with our choices." At last she gave up on the toast and set her fork down on her plate. "Since we can't always have what we want—"

"Zoe, I'm just about ready to leave if you are, so... Oh. Sorry." Now dressed in a beige cowl-necked sweater and wool slacks, Brianna stood with her hand braced against the pushed-open kitchen door, the baby slung on her hip. "Did I barge in at an inopportune time?"

"Not at all," Zoe said, rising from the table. While her voice was steady, it was strained. Perhaps he'd cracked open that can of worms after all. "I'm finished. Just need to use the bathroom and get my purse and we can go." Without another word, or even so much as a glance in his direction, she gathered her dishes into a neat stack and carried them into the kitchen.

Not surprisingly, Brianna was in the dining room not two seconds after Zoe was out of it. She plopped down in the chair Zoe had just vacated, turning the baby around in her lap to face the table.

"What's going on?" she asked, one hand efficiently removing all breakables from the toddler's reach and handing him a silver spoon which he promptly put in his mouth.

This was not the tone of someone who routinely took her employees for granted. This was the tone of a she-tiger who wouldn't think twice about disemboweling anyone who dared to mess with one of her cubs. But Mike wasn't going to sidestep the issue.

"Zoe's overworked and exhausted. But she won't admit it."

Brianna sighed deeply, rubbing the space between her eyes. "I know she is. And, before you go accusing me of her condition being my fault, it probably is. To a certain extent." She gave a soft laugh. "Close your mouth, Mr. Kwan. The startled look doesn't suit you."

"Why—?"

"Don't tell me you've never inadvertently overworked your assistant, because I wouldn't believe you. We've been swamped, both with the salon business and now this. Zoe is brilliant at organization and detail, which you may or may not have picked up. I can throw things at her and she fixes them. Always. And up until a few months ago, she seemed to thrive on it. In fact, there have been times when I've had to force her to take a vacation or an afternoon off, because she was afraid I'd screw something up in her absence. But she's been...I don't know. Preoccupied, discontented..." She frowned, shaking her head. "Unhappy. Since her birthday, it seems. And I haven't a single clue why. She may be terrific at solving other people's problems, but she sure doesn't talk about her own. Never has."

The tall woman stood up from the table, snuggling her child to her chest. "Trust me, Mike. The last thing I want to do is run Zoe into the ground. She seems to be doing that all by herself. So..." She hesitated, skimming her fingertip over the edge of one of the linen place mats, then met his gaze. "If you can get through to her, find out what's bothering her so much, my only comment is—go for it."

She started back toward the kitchen.

"Brianna?"

"Yes?" she said, one hip already pushing against the swinging door.

"You really have no idea then what's making her so unhappy?"

She shook her head. "Not really. But..."

"But...?"

"But I have a pretty good idea what she *needs*." Then, with one of those damnably enigmatic smiles that have doomed the male half of the species since the dawn of the human experience, she left the room.

As it happened, there was little they could do. The Pierre had been gracious enough to give them a small storage room where they could let the gowns hang out over the weekend, and they'd gone over the arrangements for the seating and refreshments with the events manager. But other than that, since the banquet room wouldn't be available to them until 6:00 a.m. Monday morning, their work was finished by noon.

They walked back the few blocks to the penthouse in virtual silence, Zoe studying the puffs of breath in front of her face in the sharp fall air. It was one of those days that made New Yorkers forgive the city its blistering, muggy summers, torrential spring rains and dreary, biting winters. Autumn in Manhattan bordered on being magical, but Zoe wasn't in the mood to be enchanted.

What little conversation passed between her and Brianna was related to the coming week. It was going to be tricky, both logistically and, they realized, politically. Before, when Brianna's own designs were limited to the few custom pieces she did for her own brides, she would come to Market like any other buyer, purchasing her samples from the other vendors for her salon. Now, however, she would be in direct competition with the very manufacturers who had been her suppliers for five years. It was quite possible that more than a few noses would be bent out of shape. Some vendors, in fact, might not even want to sell to her.

Zoe, for the most part, wasn't terribly concerned. "You're not going to make huge inroads in Bianchi's or Milady's business," she insisted. "Your designs are too different. We're still going to get just as many requests for the more traditional designs as ever, you know."

"You know it, and I know it—but how do we convince the other houses of that?"

"Well," Zoe said, "we'll just have to play it by ear, won't we?"

Brianna snorted. "Yeah. And pray we're not both tone-deaf."

They had come to the canopied entrance to the apartment building. Brianna touched Zoe's arm, nodding across the street toward the park.

She tucked her hands into the swing coat's deep pockets. "Let's go for a walk, kiddo. It's a gorgeous day, and since we're so early, no one's expecting us back yet."

"What about the kids?"

Brianna hitched up her shoulder bag and crossed the street, her arm linked in Zoe's. "It won't hurt them to let Colleen spoil them for another half hour. Not that they don't get enough spoiling with Edwina, but don't tell Colleen that."

Edwina Lockhart, Spencer's mother, had been instrumental in getting Spencer and Brianna together. As such, she took special pride in the grandchildren she helped, indirectly, to produce. Now *there* was a case, Zoe had to admit, where a healthy dose of judicious meddling had paid off.

She wasn't so sure, however, about the dose she suspected was about to be rammed down her throat.

"How's your sister doing?" Brianna asked. "Her due date's pretty close now, isn't it?"

Zoe knew Brianna was circling around what she wanted to say, whatever that was. But, as she was the woman's hostage, she figured she'd let the conversation take its own course for the moment.

They sidestepped a scruffy, sweat-suited man jogging with an Irish wolfhound. "She's got three weeks left. Last time I spoke with her, she was ready to spit nails."

Brianna laughed softly. "I imagine she was. The last month's worth the first eight put together."

"Even worse than morning sickness?" Zoe knew that Brianna had been miserable with Melissa during her first three months.

"Hmm. Maybe not. But you know, trite as it may be, you go through labor and heap curses on your husband's head—" the blonde's mouth curved into a gentle smile at that "—and swear you'll never, *never* go through it again. And then you see the baby…" Her voice drifted off, as did her focus. "And the awestruck expression on your husband's face, and you know you'd do it all over again." She grinned. "Okay, maybe not right at that moment, but again."

They sat on a sunny bench just outside the zoo entrance. Across from them, two little boys stood ankle-deep in the midst of a sea of gurgling pigeons, shrieking with glee as they tossed bits of bread for the mottled birds to fight over. From a collection of nearby food carts, a sudden breeze carried a whiff of roasting chestnuts, the aroma of steaming hot dogs. Zoe breathed deeply, pushing a strand of hair off her face.

"Think you might have another baby?" she asked.

Brianna leaned back against bench, studying the giggling little boys. "We've talked about it. We'd both like another child, but with our schedules…'' She shrugged. ''What you want and what makes sense are rarely the same thing. And often what you're *given* is something else apart from *that*.'' Her sigh blended with the brisk breeze wending through the trees, the Fifth Avenue traffic, the hordes of chattering parents and children streaming through the park entrance. ''You compromise, and you learn to roll with the punches, and you hang in there together and hope for the best. And learn to trust your instincts. That's about all that anyone can do.'' She looked at Zoe. '''Happily-ever-after' takes a helluva lot of work. Too many people haven't figured that out, though.''

''And…is it worth it?''

Brianna offered Zoe a confident grin, her sheer foundation unable to completely mask the dusting of freckles across her slim nose. ''What do you think?'' Then she sobered. ''What about you, kiddo?''

Zoe tensed, began to twist one of her rings around her fingers. ''What about me?''

''What's your happiness quotient these days?''

She tried a laugh. ''Been too busy to check.''

After a moment, Brianna said, her words directed to the street, ''Mike's noticed how tired and out of sorts you are. He's concerned about you.''

''Mike? What the hell business is this of his?'' Her own intensity caught her off guard.

''Nothing, I suppose,'' Brianna said placidly, running a slender hand through her windblown hair. ''He just mentioned it in passing.'' Then she nailed her with those deceptively calm eyes. ''But what is *this*, honey? Because I've noticed it, too.''

''Noticed what?''

''Your edginess lately. You've even been snapping at the ladies, which you never used to do. I've tried to cover for you—''

''You don't have to cover for me, Brianna.'' Zoe's arms pretzeled themselves across her chest. ''If I've offended one of the staff, just tell me. I'll deal with it myself.''

She could feel Brianna's gaze on the side of her face.

"Mike's absolutely right. I think you are overworked. When we get back, maybe we should think about getting a new full-time manager for the salon, so you can concentrate on the new line with me—"

"No!"

"Oh. Well...would you rather stay with the salon, then? I could start interviewing for an assistant for the line—"

"What are you saying, Brianna? That I can't handle the workload anymore?"

Brianna backed away slightly, her pale brows knotted. "That's exactly what I'm saying. I never expected you to handle both things like this. But I needed you temporarily, to get this off the ground, because I knew I could trust you. Mike made me realize, though, that I'd probably pushed it too far. You need more time to yourself, Zoe—"

"For *what?*" She had started to tremble, her body betraying the fact that Brianna was hitting far too close to home.

"For starters, how about a life? Look, when you were still in school, I remember your saying, when I was concerned about all your weekends being taken up dressing brides—remember?—I remember you said you'd take the tips for now and live your life later. Well, sweetie pie, unless I'm mistaken, 'later' came about two years ago. And you missed it."

"Oh, for crying out loud, Bree—I just turned twenty-six—"

"And your entire life revolves around other women's weddings. I've been there, Zo. I know the trap. It's deadly. And it doesn't help that your sisters are married and one of them is expecting a baby."

Zoe looked at her as if frogs were jumping out of her head. "What does that have to do with anything?"

"Plenty. Trust me. And then there's this extremely nice package of testosterone sleeping in the room next to yours."

Zoe rolled her eyes. "No thanks to you."

"Oh, no. You can thank me all you want."

She couldn't quite believe she was hearing this. "So you're saying you had an ulterior motive in asking Mike to come up with us, to stay in the apartment?'' Her eyes widened. "You're trying to push us together, aren't you?''

"Not…exactly. Let's just say…I'm just giving you the opportunity to *wake up,* for God's sake, and smell the pheromones.''

"You know…'' Zoe sprang up off the bench, her fists clenched at her sides. Her sudden movement jerked several of the pigeons into a brief, aborted flight before they fluttered back down to their feast. "I don't know about you, but I'm not enjoying this conversation very much. Why does everybody think they know more about what I need than I do? Why does everyone insist on interfering so much?''

Brianna rose, as well, laying her arm across Zoe's shoulders. "Do you know what you need, Zo?'' she asked gently.

She thought of Mike, the warmth and safety of his arms. His smile, his preposterous sense of humor. The way he looked at Brianna's children. His integrity and honesty and even the fact that he liked to cook. And her eyes swam.

"Yes,'' she said simply. "I know what I need.''

"Then what are you going to do about it?''

She sniffed, swiped at her nose with the back of her hand. "Nothing,'' she said.

"Nothing? Why—?''

"Like you said, Brianna. What you want and what makes sense are rarely the same thing.''

"So…because you can't have—or don't think you can have—what you want, you're using work as a substitute.''

"I love this job,'' Zoe said, stunned by the panic in her voice. "I don't know what I'd do without it.''

Brianna whipped her around, her hands firmly on her shoulders. Out of the corner of her eye, Zoe noticed the boys' father had taken them by the hands and moved them on. "Well, missy—listen up. If you don't figure out how to balance things a bit, and start behaving like a normal, healthy twenty-six-year-old woman, you may just get the opportunity to find out.''

"What are you saying?''

"I'm saying that I can get another assistant. I would hate it, and probably hate her, but I can do it. But I'll be damned if I'm going to sit back and watch you hide behind my business ventures because you're too chicken to get off your butt and deal with the real world!"

Zoe stood there in front of Brianna, at Fifth Avenue and Sixty-fifth Street, as hordes of tourists and noontime joggers and parents with kids swarmed around them, with her mouth hanging wide open.

"You'd *fire* me?"

She could see the pain in Brianna's face as she nodded.

"If that's what it takes to make you wake up—yes, Zoe. I'd fire you."

9

Mike was in a good mood. Hell, he was in an *exceptional* mood. The account was going to be better than he'd thought, and the owner had given him a lead for a large sporting goods retail chain with stores in twenty states. He grinned like a fool at the doorman as he showed his identification before the bear-like man would let him set foot inside the lobby.

"Have Mrs. Lockhart and Miss Chan returned yet?"

"Yes, sir," the brown-liveried man replied. "About a half hour ago. Mrs. Lockhart's gone again, though. Went out with her husband."

Privacy was apparently not real high on this guy's list. Either that, or Mike's charm was working its magic again. Whatever.

That meant Zoe was still in the apartment. With nothing to do. Except, maybe, go for a walk with him. Hey—if Colleen the Terrible would let them go, maybe they could take the kids to the zoo.

Munching on this pleasant thought like a piece of candy, he rode up the elevator, got off, punched in the code to the door, walked inside.

Silence. Deep, profound, luxury apartment silence. He smelled baking—brownies!

God, life was good. A new account, a breathtaking fall day, an even more breathtaking woman to take to dinner tonight. And brownies. Heaven in a New York penthouse.

He found Zoe in the living room, curled up in a corner of

one of the sofas, her head propped in her hand as she read a magazine. Her hair had come loose, molten coal caught between her back and the sofa.

At that moment, he almost thought he loved her. He knew the thought was probably foolish and definitely adrenaline driven, but he didn't care.

Carefully he snuck up behind her, his footsteps completely silenced by the thick Chinese rug underfoot. Then, like a cat pouncing on a bird, he swept down on her, enclosing her shoulders in a hug as he pulled her back against him and planted a kiss on her right temple.

She shrieked, the magazine flying out of her hands as she catapulted off the sofa, banging her knee against the coffee table in front of it.

"What the *hell* do you think you're doing?" Her voice was a fierce whisper; he at once realized the children must be taking their naps.

"I'm really sorry...." Damn. "That was stupid of me, Zoe. I apologize." He gestured lamely toward her knee. "Are you okay?"

"Considering I probably just cracked my shinbone, no, I'm not." Her eyes were shimmering with tears as she rubbed her injured leg.

He stepped around the sofa and held out his hands. "Here...sit down a minute—"

"Just...get away from me," she said quietly, smacking at the tear that tracked down her cheek.

"Zoe, honey—I'm sorry. I certainly didn't mean for you to get hurt."

He saw her haul in a breath large enough to fill a dirigible. "I'm not talking about my leg. I'm talking about..." She paused, and he could actually see her fill up with anger, like pouring toxic chemicals into a beaker until they bubbled out the top. "What business is it of yours to talk to Brianna about me? What gives you the right to stick your nose into my affairs? You hardly even know me."

He pulled away a little, at a loss. "All I did was make an offhand comment that I thought you looked tired."

"Some offhand comment," she muttered. "Now she's convinced that maybe I'm overdoing it, that maybe the job's even bad for my mental, physical and emotional well-being. So she's threatening to let me go."

"*What?*"

"Yeah. Ain't that a kicker? A job I've busted my butt for over the last four years, that I've sacrificed everything for. A five-minute conversation with you, and it could all go down the tubes."

"That doesn't make sense. Brianna worships you, Zoe. She said herself she can count on you for anything. Why on earth would she want to fire you?"

"Well, Michael, since you and she have become such buddies, maybe you could find out for me and let me know. Now, if you'll excuse me," she said, bending over and retrieving the splayed magazine, "I was in the middle of a fascinating article on killer whales...."

"Can it, Zoe," he said, ripping the magazine out of her hands and forcibly sitting her down on the sofa. "Now, I don't know what the hell all this is about, and I sure don't know how a passing comment got so screwed up, but we're going to talk." Feeling rash, he touched her cheek. "Or make out. The choice is yours."

He'd had no idea her eyes could get so big. If nothing else, he'd managed to stun her speechless. Not an easy task, he surmised.

Predictably, she tried to bolt. He held her fast.

"So...what'll it be? Talking or necking?"

Now the eyes narrowed. "I think I hate you."

"I'll take that risk. So?"

*Un*predictably, she hesitated before her answer. "Talking."

"Not the choice I would have made," he said with a rueful grin, "but I'm not surprised."

She grunted.

"Now." He patted her hand like a patient uncle. "What, exactly, did Brianna say?"

As best she could, Zoe recounted the conversation in the park. Mike held her hands the whole time, his fingers gently stroking hers. He commented little, but the pressure of his warm, strong hands against hers communicated plenty. Ten minutes into the conversation she'd almost regretted not taking the other choice.

"Okay," he said at last, letting go of her hands. Missing his immediately, she folded hers into her lap. "Let's see if I got this straight. Brianna thinks you're working too hard, right?"

"I guess—"

"And she also thinks you're so wrapped up in your job that you're neglecting other aspects of your life."

She nodded and pressed her hands more tightly together.

"So, her ultimatum was, if I understand you correctly, is that either she sees some change along those lines, or she's going to fire you. For your own good."

Another nod.

"Okay…" Mike got up, wandered over to the fireplace, one hand in his pocket, pensively stroking his bottom lip. "And then there're your sisters…" he said, almost more to himself than her.

"My…sisters?"

He turned. "Yeah. Bugging you to go out with this what's-his-name."

"Oh. Right." She sighed. "I told them I would, to get them off my case. I have no intention of following through, but I'll deal with that when the time comes."

"What…*is* his name? For the sake of…argument."

Now she laughed, for the first time since her conversation with Brianna. "You're not going to believe this, but I have no idea. Margi told me, but there was a birthday party going on behind us…." She waved her hand. "Doesn't matter anyway. You were saying?"

He began pacing the room, slowly, rubbing the base of his neck. "Well...now this is a wild shot, granted. But it might be worth it. Say you were to go out with me...."

She frowned, following his movement across the room. "You mean...like having dinner with you tonight?"

"Sure. That'd do. For starters, anyway..."

"For...starters?"

He had apparently not heard her. "But say, you made it seem more...real. Like we had something going." Then he faced her, only to laugh at what must have been her flabbergasted expression. "Oh, come on, now...it's not that preposterous an idea, is it?"

Frankly she wasn't sure what sort of an idea it was. But *preposterous* would do.

Intriguing wasn't a bad choice, either.

"Go on," she said.

"Well, if Brianna and your sisters at least *thought* you were dating—getting on with your life—maybe they would leave you alone. Brianna would see you could do your job and still have a personal life, and your sisters wouldn't push you about dating this whoever he is. See?"

She saw. She saw the merits, certainly, in such a scheme. But the pitfalls, too. And there were pitfalls aplenty.

"How...far would we carry this little charade?"

He seemed to hesitate. "Just far enough to convince everyone who needs convincing," he said, and a chill scuttled up her spine.

This was like being handed fifty-yard-line seats to the Super Bowl. Of course, that doesn't necessarily mean you have to actually use the tickets—but what fool wouldn't?

Mike had never believed in chance or luck or fortune, good or bad. Until he met Zoe. Now, as he watched a succession of unlikely pieces continue to fall into place, he wondered.

She'd agreed to his idea, but he wasn't kidding himself into believing it was for any other reason than the ones he'd brought up—to keep Brianna and her sisters at bay.

So he took her to dinner, as planned, then pushed his luck with a movie, too. She didn't protest. Nor did she protest his suggestion of coffee afterward. Two hours and three cups of coffee each later, they were still arguing good-naturedly about the film. And at least a dozen others, as well.

Whether Zoe would admit it or not, she was beginning to relax. The lines around her mouth had vanished, and her eyes no longer had that dusty look. And she was good for him, too. She teased him mercilessly and made him laugh out loud and made him forget, when he was with her, everything *but* her.

It felt good. Damn good.

But for how long? After all, they weren't operating in real time while they were here. Here, in New York, away from the day-to-day...*stuff* that devoured his life, he could fit her in. Go to dinner or catch a movie without feeling guilty or wondering what phone calls he was missing. Once back in Atlanta, though...

This really was just pretend. And he'd better damn sight remember that. Luck would only go so far, after all.

He nodded toward the front of the coffee shop as he picked up the check. "I guess we better get out of here before they kick us out. That waitress is giving me the evil eye."

"Oh." Zoe glanced over her shoulder at the glowering redhead. "Mmm. I see your point." She grabbed her purse. "Guess we better."

The frigid air nipped their cheeks when they stepped out of the diner. They started to walk back, but after a minute Mike noticed Zoe clutching her peacoat collar around her throat.

"Cold?" he asked.

"L-let's put it this way," she stammered. "I can't feel my ears anymore, and it's just been one block."

"Let's get a cab, then—" He stepped out to hail one.

"No." She put her hand on his arm, pulled him back. "I'd rather walk."

He turned, looked down into her face. "Even though you're freezing."

She nodded. Then did an excellent imitation of a freezing puppy.

Was this another gift? Or a trick of fate? He glanced at her small, shivering form two feet away. And made a choice.

He slipped his arm around her shoulders, and she simply molded herself to his side.

"This is…just because you're cold, you understand," he said, afraid to trust. To believe that what he felt at this moment could possibly last past these enchanted few days.

Afraid he would forget he was supposed to be pretending.

Afraid he already had.

"Of course," she said stiffly. From the cold, he presumed.

They walked in silence the rest of the way.

Well, if nothing else, they had fun together, Zoe thought as she let Mike help her off with her coat when they got inside. As charades went, this one was probably better than most. She just had to remind herself—repeatedly, if necessary—that men didn't share the same romantic notions of things that women did. He probably really meant it, when he said he was just putting his arm around her to keep her warm.

Pity she didn't feel the same way. But that wasn't his fault, and she wasn't going to make an issue out of it. He'd offered his services, as it were, and she accepted the offer fully aware of the terms and limitations under which it had been offered. It was no good trying to change the contract now. And she knew that. She did.

"Hot chocolate?" he asked, nodding toward the kitchen as he hitched up his sweater sleeves.

She laughed, then whispered, "After all that coffee? I'll be up four times tonight as it is."

He chuckled. "Keep me company while I have some, then."

It was a gentle command, easily ignored. But she couldn't have, she realized, even if she wanted to.

They were surprised to find Brianna in the kitchen, sitting at the table in her forest green velour robe, a cup of something hot clutched in her fingers. Even at one in the morning, she exuded elegance.

Zoe smirked, one hand going to her hip. "Hmmph. Waiting up for me, were you?"

Brianna pulled her mouth tight. "Please. Just couldn't sleep, worrying about the show, and the other vendors..." She waved away her concerns, then took a sip of her tea. "So...what did you see?"

That led to a reprise of their marathon argument while Mike fixed his hot chocolate.

"I'm sorry," he said. "I just can't see Eastwood in that part. He's a fine actor, but why play a character twenty years younger?" He settled into a chair at Brianna's right, sitting sideways so his long legs could stretch out into the kitchen.

Zoe straddled the chair opposite, her arms folded across the top. "Because nobody cares, that's why—"

"I care—"

"Doesn't count. You're a man."

Mike looked to Brianna for support. "Is she always like this?"

"Uh, yeah. Pretty much." Then, with an impish smile, she leaned toward Mike. "Let me give you a piece of advice, though."

"What's that?" he said, snagging Zoe's eyes in his.

Laying one hand on his arm, Brianna said in a stage whisper, "You'll get farther if you let her win."

Uh-kay. That's it, folks. Her cheeks suddenly flaming, Zoe pushed off the chair. "Well, it's late, so I think I'm going to turn in...." She watched, her stomach fluttering, as Mike got up from his chair and walked around the table toward her. She backed up a step, rammed her hip into the corner of the counter.

He stopped in front of her, leaned over, kissed her softly on the lips. Simply, sweetly, quickly. Didn't even touch her, except to tap her on the nose. "See you in the morning," he said with a smile, then returned to his seat.

Her heart thunking in her chest, Zoe caught Brianna's wink

and smile, before she managed to get out of the kitchen and to her room without falling over.

"So...indulge me," Mike heard from the other side of the kitchen the following morning as he fixed brunch for the two of them. Brianna and Spencer had taken the children to the Natural History Museum, Colleen had gone to church. "What was that all about last night?"

Mike pivoted to her, then turned back to his omelette. "What was what all about?"

"Don't be coy, Michael. It doesn't suit you. That kiss."

He was being coy, wasn't he? Considering how to answer, he folded over the puffy omelette, then let his eyes drift to her face. She met his gaze directly, fearlessly, her arms crossed over her chest.

"I just thought it might lend credence to our...story."

"Oh. Of course."

She quickly picked up her coffee cup, and he felt a prick in his heart.

He'd gone and done it now, hadn't he? He hated this "pretending," but how could he tell her the truth? What good would it do to confess that he wanted to kiss her for the simple, primitive reason that he wanted to see what kissing her was like while he had the chance? How could he tell her that, had Brianna *not* been present, the kiss would have been a helluva lot more than a peck on the lips?

How could he tell her he was falling in love with her in one breath, only to insist it wouldn't work in the next?

He slipped the omelette onto her plate, then sat down. Wondered how he'd get his own breakfast past the knot in his stomach.

"Look," he exhaled. "Maybe this whole...thing is a mistake."

Her empty cup rattled in the saucer as she put it down. "What whole thing?"

"Our...ruse. I mean, it's not as if we can keep it up.

Brianna and your sisters would just find out anyway. Then what?''

Zoe took a bite of her toast and eyed him wordlessly for several seconds as she chewed. Then she swallowed and asked softly, ''Michael Kwan…are you backing out on me?''

He frowned. This wasn't what he expected. But then, *Zoe* wasn't what he expected. Or ever would be, he imagined.

''I just thought—''

''That I was taking things too seriously? That something was going to happen that we didn't plan?'' Before he could answer, she got up and fetched the coffeepot from its stand. ''You really must do something about your inflated ego, you know.'' She poured herself coffee, topped off his cup. ''It's beginning to get on my nerves.''

''I don't…'' He shook his head. ''When you just asked me what had happened last night—''

Zoe straightened up and looked him in the eye, her eyebrows lifted. ''Oh…that?'' She shrugged. ''I was just curious. Besides, as long as I'm in this game, I want to be absolutely clear that we're playing by the same rules. That's all.''

''So…you didn't read anything more into my actions last night.''

Having set the pot back on its base, she reseated herself at the table, replacing her napkin on her lap. ''Don't be ridiculous, Mike. Of course not. I was just checking on *you.*'' She took a sip of her coffee. ''So…what should we do today? How about the Met?''

''Even though Brianna won't be around all day? I mean, there's no reason to—''

''Pretend? No, I don't suppose there is. But there's no reason for the two of us to spend all day cooped up in this apartment, either.''

For a second—a long, uncomfortably warm second—an exquisitely detailed image of how they might keep each other entertained all day in the apartment sprang to mind.

He bit off a large chunk of toast. ''Fine,'' he mumbled around his full mouth. ''The museum's fine.''

"Perfect," she said. "And by the way—" she lifted up a forkful of omelette "—this is to die for. If I dare say that without your head getting any fatter than it already is."

"I'll try to keep it in perspective," he grumbled, deciding he didn't have the energy to figure her out.

She'd had no choice but to go on the offensive. Throw him off guard. Zoe wasn't going to be any man's victim anymore, wittingly or otherwise. Like she said, as long as everybody played by the same rules, she'd be fine.

So for the next three days, that's what she told herself. Unfortunately, instead of feeling on top of the situation, she felt as if she was being dragged into it deeper and deeper. By Wednesday, Mike's last night in New York, she was about two inches away from becoming a basket case.

Now, workwise, things couldn't have been better. Monday's and Tuesday's shows went off without a hitch, no one gave Zoe any grief when she showed up at the other vendors' shows, and Brianna was taking in orders like mad. In fact, Brianna was so tired, she said it was just as well Spencer had returned to Atlanta on Monday, because she hardly had the *oomph* to talk to her children in the evenings, let alone be a wife. Yeah, workwise, things were just peachy-keeno.

Lifewise was something else again.

She and Mike had spent Sunday together, as well as Monday evening. He'd been friendly and kind and attentive, but distant. There had been no more kisses—she presumed since Brianna wasn't around to witness—and almost no touching. Okay, so maybe he was playing by the rules. But Zoe wasn't real sure she liked them anymore.

Tuesday, she'd begged off, too tired to see or be with anyone. But Mike had extracted a promise from her that she'd go out with him Wednesday evening, no matter what. At this point, as she and Brianna hobbled back to the apartment at six, all she could think was, "Why?" Why did he keep asking her out? And why did she keep accepting?

They sank onto the sofas in the living room as a pair of

curly-headed locomotives clamored over each of them in turn. Zoe allowed a hug and kiss for each of "her" children, vaguely wondering how on earth mothers did this every day. How could you come home, ready to drop, and deal with these demanding little critters jumping around, yammering your ears off? Then she watched Brianna, who she knew was every bit as tired as she was, stroking Tyler's head as he cuddled against her stomach, smiling for Melissa as she recited a new nursery rhyme she'd learned that day.

There was no epiphanous flash of understanding, no sudden "aha!". Brianna's forehead was creased and her smile was weary, and, except for caressing her baby's head, she barely moved. But she did it. She had the kids there, with her, and when Colleen came to drag them off to their dinners, Brianna dragged herself off the sofa, as well, and followed her children into the kitchen. Unlike other mothers who didn't have the luxury of nannies and housekeepers, she could have taken the easy way out. But she didn't.

"Will you be taking dinner here this evening, Miss Zoe?" Colleen asked, paused in the doorway.

She shook her head. "This is Mike's last night. I told him I'd go out with him." She winced, rubbing her instep. "Which was my second mistake."

"And what was your first?" the housekeeper said with a chuckle.

"Buying these damn shoes." She picked up the high-vamped black velvet heels and grimaced as Colleen left the room. "What was I thinking?" she muttered to herself.

"I always find," a low voice washed over her from the other side of the room, "when it comes to women's shoes, *thought* doesn't seem to enter into it." Wearing a geometrically patterned sweater in a mix of grays and beiges, Mike sat on the sofa beside her and took one of the torture devices in his hand. "Now, I ask you..." He held the shoe out toward her. "Does this make a drop of sense?"

"Oh, shut up," Zoe said, swiping the thing out of his hand. Mike patted his lap. "Swing those little tootsies up here."

She pulled back, suspicious. "Why?"

"Ever have a foot massage?"

Cautiously, she shook her head.

"Some people think it's better than chocolate. Or sex," he added calmly, not even looking at her as he positioned her stockinged foot on his lap. The second he started to work on her instep, she groaned, collapsing against the arm of the sofa.

"Were they right?"

She forced her mouth to work. "Was who right?"

"About this being better than chocolate?"

"It's too close to call," she said on another groan.

"What about the other?"

"Keep going. I'll let you know." This was already better than any sex *she'd* ever had. Which led her to wonder—if Mike was this good at *this,* how good would he be at *that?*

She shut her eyes over his low chuckle, drifting into the rhythm of his talented fingers soothing, kneading, stroking…. She dozed off for a few seconds, jerked herself awake to find his eyes riveted to hers.

She'd have to be completely blind not to see the desire behind them. Controlled desire, which made it somehow more dangerous. Something had just shifted, she thought. The rules had changed again, but no one had given her a copy of the new ones.

"Wh-what are you doing?" she asked, feeling a little drugged.

"Making you feel better, I hope," he said softly.

She pulled her foot away. "Maybe we shouldn't be doing this."

Half his mouth lifted into a smile. "Doing what? I'm giving you a massage. *You're* not doing anything except falling asleep." He patted her ankles. "Which is just what you should be doing so you're fresh to go out this evening."

This evening. *Oy.*

"Mike, I'm so tired…."

"I know you are, honey, but…" He lowered his voice to a

conspiratorial whisper. "How is it going to look if we don't spend the last night I'm here together?"

"Like I'm too tired to go out," she retorted. "For goodness' sake, I'll be back in Atlanta on Saturday. We...we don't have to carry this thing *too* far, you know."

He pulled her other foot up onto his lap and started working his magic. The thought crossed her mind that if he tried—and not even that hard, she suspected—to seduce her, she'd be in serious trouble. With great effort, she pulled her foot away, tucking both of them under her.

"This is too intimate, Mike."

His brows lifted. "It's a foot massage, Zoe. Since when can't a friend give another friend a foot massage?"

When they make the other friend feel all goony and dangerously close to losing control, she thought.

"It's...just making me nervous, okay?"

He smiled, and she went all soft and jiggly inside, so much so a fluttery little laugh bubbled out of her throat.

"What's so funny?" He stroked her arm where it lay stretched across the back of the sofa.

"Nothing. I think I'm hungry. I'm getting light-headed."

"Ready for dinner, then?"

She wasn't ready. For dinner or anything else.

"Sure," she said.

Dinner, at least, was fine. That, and the cold, moist air swirling around them even perked her up enough to take a short walk—in her flats—afterward. Shortly after they began to walk, however, she realized she was cold. Mike realized it, too. And once again he put his arm around her shoulders.

Just to keep her warm, she told herself. That's all.

"That better?" he said over her head, his breath—his lips?—grazing her hair.

She nodded.

"This...has been fun," he said. Almost cautiously, she thought.

"Yeah. It has."

"Think we convinced Brianna?"

She pulled away from him, ostensibly to check out a store window.

He joined her. "That would look nice on you," he said softly, eyeing the beaded turquoise evening gown on the single mannequin.

With a sharp laugh, she started up the street toward Fifth. "Like I'd have anywhere to wear something like that." Cold again, she rammed her gloved hands into her coat pocket and refused to let her teeth chatter.

His long legs easily caught up to her. He snagged her arm with his hand, pulled her companionably close.

"So, Miss Zoe...what do you want? A brilliant career? Wealth?" He paused. "A devoted hubby and a dozen kids?"

The answer was surprisingly clear. And stabbed her to the core.

You, she thought, then shoved the thought away, like an underfoot puppy.

"I don't know," she said with a shrug. "To be happy, I suppose."

He turned her to him, and in the clear-as-day glow from the street lamps and shop windows, the set of his mouth stole her breath. And she wanted—so much!—to touch his face, his lips. To lift herself up on tiptoe and mate her mouth with his.

She swallowed.

And licked her lips.

"You shouldn't do that in this cold," he whispered, smoothing his thumb over her mouth, wicking away the dampness. "Your lips will get chapped."

"They...they were dry," she said. Hoarsely.

"There's a better way to moisten them," he said, and her knees went weak.

"I hate Chap Stick."

"Glad to hear it," he said, moving imperceptibly closer. "You know, if this were a real date, and if we weren't just...pretending, I'd probably do this—" his lips grazed hers, gently, tantalizingly "—right about now."

"But…this isn't a real date," she said, beginning to tremble.

"Well, why don't we pretend it is?"

That was the moment the world went nuts. Her world, anyway. It spun and danced and tilted, making her deliciously dizzy with the feel of his mouth on hers. His lips met hers in a dance both gentle and frantic, his mouth hot and soft and seeking, his hands cradling her face as he kissed her, and kissed her again, deeply, desperately, until she wasn't sure she could stand or breathe or think coherently and she didn't bloody care.

If he'd asked her to bed at that moment, "No" would not have been her first response.

And that made tears spring to her eyes, because, if she'd accepted, then what? An affair? For how long? Until he realized he was spending too much time with her, that she was interfering with his work, that he was neglecting his business because of her?

She'd already been screwed, literally and figuratively, by one bastard who had considered her just one love of many. She was damned if she was going to let that happen a second time.

"Zoe—baby?" Mike's fingers swept away a tear. "What's the matter?"

I love you, you turkey, she thought angrily. "Why did you do that?" Bitterness flooded her thoughts, her words. "We're just supposed to be pretending."

"Is that what you thought I was doing?" he asked.

Confused, she searched his eyes. "Weren't you?"

"Sure seemed pretty real to me."

"Yeah," she said, twisting out of his arms and storming up the street. "'*Seemed*' is the perfect word, isn't it?"

"Zoe, look—"

She whirled on him so fast she nearly bumped her nose into his chest. "This 'game' has gone far enough. I must have been a real idiot to think I could do this," she muttered to herself, then met his gaze as unflinchingly as she could. "Was this part of the 'plan'? Some Freudian theory that maybe I just needed a good toss in the hay to square me away?''

"Zoe! You're being ridiculous—''

"I am *never* ridiculous! Stubborn, yes. But never ridiculous. Ask anyone who's ever known me. Zoe the predictable. Zoe the logical. Zoe the reliable.'' She was crying now, unable to stop the torrent streaming down her cheeks. "I don't do things like…like…'' She gestured helplessly at the space between them.

"Then what *do* you do? Do you keep running every time something comes up that might be remotely dangerous? Do you hide out in your apartment, afraid to risk whatever it is you're afraid to risk, for fear of getting hurt?''

"I *have* been hurt, Michael!'' she yelled, then forced herself to lower her voice. "And I didn't like it a whole helluva lot. And since I'm not like other women who can't seem to learn from their mistakes—being the logical one here—I have no desire to go through that again.''

"What *do* you want, Zoe?'' he asked again.

She jerked out of his arms and walked away, her hands straining against the lining in her pockets. She thought and argued with herself—and with the little critter still wondering if it was time to come out yet—until she turned, walked back up to Mike and glared right into those luminous black eyes.

"You,'' she said, aloud this time, surprised at how steady her voice was. "I want *you*. But not under these conditions, or whatever half-assed terms you seem to think I'd be willing to settle for.'' When he didn't reply, she shook her head and began walking back to the apartment.

"Zoe—'' he called behind her. She heard his footsteps as he ran to catch up.

"Go away,'' she said. "Just go the hell away. All I want is to go back to the apartment, go to my room and pretend none of this ever happened.''

"Honey, you can't walk alone—''

"Oh, for Chr—'' She stopped, faced him. "I've been to New York before. I can take care of myself, which no one seems to believe. Besides, there are five doormen per square foot along here. Just…leave me alone, okay?''

As she walked away, she heard behind her, ''What about when we get back to Atlanta? About your sisters?''

She turned, walking backward. ''I suppose I'll be meeting David Wu's grandson soon,'' she said, then shrugged. ''Why not, huh?''

She managed to hold on to most of the rage until she got back to the apartment, where she was grateful to discover that Brianna had gone to bed early, leaving Zoe free to cry herself to sleep.

Somehow, he'd figured victory would have tasted sweeter. Hadn't she said she wanted him? Hadn't she made it plain just how strong her feelings were? Isn't this what he wanted? What he *thought* he wanted?

But she'd smacked the ball back into his court with the force of a bullet. This was no ''let's see how things go'' situation. She'd made that plain enough. It was all or nothing. Love me or get the hell out of my way and let me get on with my life, thank you.

He wouldn't have expected anything less from her.

Or wanted it.

But…

But.

He sagged onto a park bench, dropping his head into his hands, mentally rehearsing a string of choice words he hadn't used since college.

His loving her wasn't even a question. Hadn't been, he realized, since lunch that day in the deli. But could he be what she wanted? What she needed? Could he now, somehow, juggle the demands of his business enough to satisfy a woman who deserved no less than his full attention?

He knew what she meant, too. He was sure she'd never expect him to be home at six every evening, never to work weekends, never to be out of town. But she would expect—and rightfully—that the agency wouldn't share a pillow with them in bed. That he'd be there for the soccer games and recitals and school plays—

Oh, *God!*

He shot up from the bench as if it was spring-loaded, ramming his hands through his hair with such urgency that a couple walking by swung out closer to the curb as they passed.

How much do you want her? sounded a little voice he'd never heard before.

He touched his fingers to his lips, sighed.

The answer to that question was simple: more than he'd ever wanted anything in his life.

The answer to the logical next question—what was he going to do about it?—was anything but.

10

—————◄——————

"So, you're really going out on this date tonight?" Brianna efficiently gathered up cake-and-ice-cream-smeared Barbie birthday plates from the dining room table, dumping them into a large Hefty bag in her right hand. She held up a matching cup, pulled her lips down into an expression of pure disgust. "I absolutely loathe Barbie. Why do I do this?"

Zoe laughed, replacing the half-eaten cake in its bakery box. "Because you love your daughter, and what can it hurt?"

"Other than my aesthetic sensibilities?" She shuddered and dumped more plates into the bag. "So…this date. What's his name?"

"Boy, lady—you sure know how to spoil a person's afternoon." She licked chocolate frosting off her fingers, then said, "Michael."

Brianna nearly dropped the bag. "Oh, no…"

"Cute, huh? Must be my karma this year. There was one year, I remember, when I dated three Roberts. I seem to go through them in clumps."

"Well, maybe this one will be—"

But Zoe held up one hand. "Brianna. Please. Remember who you're talking to."

Brianna swept all the crumbs off the table onto the last plate, then dumped it into the bag. Outside, they could hear a dozen little girls all under the age of six chasing Spencer around the yard. Brianna walked over to the window, chuckling. "I doubt whether that man, ever, in his wildest dreams, thought the day would come when he'd play tag with a bunch of little girls.'' She looked at Zoe. ''Just goes to show we never know what life has in store for us.''

Zoe nodded, then felt a peculiar pang in the center of her chest. As if she knew, Brianna said, ''I'm sorry about Mike. I was so sure the two of you were going to hit it off.''

''You know,'' Zoe said, pulling her shoulders back. ''I never did. Not really. Oh, the attraction was there, but...''

''Zoe?''

She faced Brianna. ''What?''

''Cut the bull. You're hurting. And it's okay to let some people know you're hurting, you know? So you're not perfect.'' She leaned on the table. ''This isn't news, I hate to tell you.''

''What? That I fell for another jerk?''

Brianna shook her head. ''Mike's not a jerk. You said yourself, he never even asked you to sleep with him. That's no jerk, sweetie.''

''No, it just means he wasn't attracted enough to even ask.''

''Oh, for the love of Pete, Zoe!'' Brianna huffed a sigh. ''There's no winning with you, is there? If he'd asked you to go to bed, he'd have been scum. Since he didn't, that meant he didn't like you enough so he's *still* scum. Here's a piece of unsolicited advice, honey. Give the guy—and yourself—a break already. It didn't work out. Period. It happens. No one's to blame, no one's at fault. It's just one of those things. Which doesn't make it hurt any less, before you jump down my throat. But there's no villain here, okay? Can you accept that?''

Zoe drifted over to the window and watched the game for a moment, her arms tucked against her ribs. ''Since when did you get to be so wise, lady?'' she asked.

''Think it happened when I gave birth the first time. Of course, they say that when the kids become teenagers, all that wisdom sort of leaks out. But, hey—I figure I'll make the best of it while I can.''

Zoe nodded, then watched Spencer toss his giggling daughter into the air, catch her, drive her into squeals of glee as he growled and nuzzled her neck.

Happiness, she mused, had to be more than just dumb luck. It had to be, at least in part, a matter of choice, as well. Maybe it had been pure chance that brought Brianna and Spencer together, that had led Spencer's sister to choose Brianna to plan her wedding, that had made Spencer the one to make the initial arrangements since Kelly had been out of town. But Brianna and Spencer had then *chosen* to be together, to stay together, to work around their hectic life-styles to accommodate each other and their beautiful children.

Perhaps there isn't any choice about who you love or don't love, she reflected, but you sure as hell have a choice what to do about it. Or try to do about it, anyway.

Just as life offered other choices, as well.

"Bree?"

"Mmm?"

"I have something to tell you." She glanced over at Brianna, whose brows were lifted in mild curiosity. "Yesterday afternoon, a woman came into the salon. Middle-aged, beautifully dressed but not flashy, you know? Classy. I figured she was probably there to see about her daughter's wedding, maybe look for a mother-of-the-bride gown, something like that. However, she introduced herself as Deirdre Swann, said she'd been a bridal consultant and manager at Sherwood's in Charleston."

The brows slid up another notch. "Sherwood's? They're *huge.*" Then they dipped. "*Had been?* As in past tense? I don't understand…"

"Her husband's just been transferred here. She came in on the off chance that you were hiring."

"Oh, dear. A woman of her caliber and experience…" Brianna sank onto one of the dining chairs. "I doubt she'd be very happy just selling gowns—"

"Um…I thought maybe…managing the salon might be more suitable." She looked up into one of the more startled expressions she'd ever seen. "What do you think?"

After a moment, Brianna said in a low voice, "I think I'm glad I'm already sitting down." She seemed to be having trouble making her mouth work. "Are you telling me you want to quit?"

"God, no!" Zoe laughed, then sat beside her employer. "But I've been thinking a lot about what you said, about needing to carve out some personal time for myself. Decided maybe it was time I took some cooking classes, 'cause I'm getting *real* tired of Healthy Choice. Maybe some gardening classes, too—"

"You? Gardening?"

She shrugged. "It's an option, right? Anyway, maybe I have been using the job as a reason to ignore the rest of the world. A little. So...I decided that you could have me *either* to run the salon and the consultancy end of things, *or* as your assistant for the line. Not both."

"I see." Brianna's mouth twitched at the corners. "And...that's your decision, huh?"

"Yep."

"And...my druthers aren't really a consideration here?"

"'Fraid not." But her voice faltered.

Brianna beamed, her arms swinging out to give Zoe a big hug. "Oh, honey," she said, holding her away, "I'm so proud of you."

"Not mad?"

"Mad? Why on earth would I be mad? If I'd be ticked off about anything, it's that it took you so damn long to figure this out." She laughed. "Don't you see? That's what I was trying to suggest in New York. Then you went all nuts on me—"

"Hey!"

Brianna waved away her objection and barreled ahead. "—and I couldn't get a word in edgewise."

"I see. So you decided to go for broke and threaten to fire me instead."

"Something like that." Then she grinned. "Apparently it worked."

Zoe snorted, got up from the table. "Okay, you can wipe the smug look off your face. Anyway, I couldn't make up my mind which I wanted to do. Then this Mrs. Swann came in, and the decision seemed to have been made for me." She turned, leaned on the edge of the table. "Wait until you meet her, Bree. She's absolutely perfect. Looked me right in the eye when we talked, smooth as glass. And her kids are grown. One daughter is an accountant, been going with the same guy all her life, one makes dolls and has three kids. There's a third one, too, a lawyer, I think she said. But anyway, weekends aren't a problem and her husband's used to it.... What's so funny?"

Brianna was laughing. "And I suppose she knows all about Margi's pregnancy and Vanessa's recent marriage by now, too?"

A flush warmed her cheeks. "We did sort of hit it off, I guess."

"Well, she sounds terrific. You'll have to set up an interview—"

"Monday afternoon at two. Is that okay?"

With a sigh, Brianna just shook her head. "Yeah. Monday at two is fine. Although..."

Zoe lifted a brow. "What?"

"I had thought that maybe you'd like to manage the New York showroom. With the response we got from the shows and the mailing, I can justify having a year-round showroom up there...."

"Thanks, but I'll pass."

"Oh...okay. But why?"

"Because this is my home. Near my meddlesome family and my honorary niece and nephew. Besides, I hate New York."

"Any particular reason?"

"Any city with that many Chinese restaurants is *not* someplace I want to live."

The front doorbell rang. Brianna flicked a glance at the clock on the mantel. "That'll be the first of the other parents come to retrieve their little princesses." She rose, automatically adjusting her skirt, smoothing her hair, assuming her lady-of-the-manor demeanor. Zoe inwardly smiled. The role suited her. Spencer suited her. As did her chaotic life-style.

Choices. It all came down to choices.

"I'd better be going, too," she said. "Need time to rev up for this date."

As they walked out to the front door, Brianna asked, "So...I'm curious. Why did you let your sisters talk you into this?"

Zoe came to a halt. "I could have said 'no,'" she said, a little amazed. "But I didn't. I *chose* to go along with this." She shook her head and continued walking. "I'm sure there's a reason, but damned if I know what it is."

She gave Brianna a quick hug, smiled an even quicker hello to Mrs. Wyman and walked out to her car. Her little voice had been quiet for the past week, chastened, she supposed, by the fiasco with Mike. Now, suddenly, there it was again, a faint, scrabbling sound.

"Maybe this one is *the one,"* it said.

"Yeah, right," she muttered to herself, maneuvering her Ford Escort around the half-dozen luxury cars pulling into the graveled, circular drive fronting the Lockhart mansion. "And I'm driving this car because the Caddy's in the shop."

The little voice had nothing to say to that.

"Thanks for coming in this afternoon, Fran," Mike said as he slipped on his topcoat. "I know you hate to work on Saturdays."

She grinned. "Just tell it to my paycheck, Michael," she said, shrugging into her own coat and picking up her purse. "So...what are your plans for tonight? And don't you dare tell me 'working.'"

"Nope. Got a date."

Her purse thudded back onto her desk. "As in, with a woman and everything?"

He waggled his brows. "I don't know about the *and everything* part, but definitely with a woman."

"My God. I think I need my blood pressure medicine."

Mike frowned. "Since when do you take blood pressure medicine?"

"I don't. Yet. Working with you may make me start, though. So...who is she?"

He grinned. Sheepishly. "Zoe."

"Chan?"

"Uh, yeah."

Her face glowed. "You mean you got back together? That's wonderf—"

"Not yet."

Now her face crumpled. "What do you mean, not yet? How can you be going out with her if you haven't gotten back together with her?"

"Because she isn't expecting me to show up."

Fran dropped back into her desk chair. "What have you been smoking, Michael? What on earth are you talking about?"

"See...Zoe's expecting David Wu's grandson to come pick her up for a blind date. But she's not expecting *me.*"

"But...you *are* David Wu's grandson. The only one living in Atlanta, anyway."

"Ah...but Zoe doesn't know that."

At that point, Fran blew out a frustrated sigh and flung her hands up into the air. Pushing herself out of her chair, she hauled her handbag off the desk once again. "Something tells me, the more I try to understand, the more confused I'm going to get. God didn't give me that many brain cells. So...well..." She crossed to the office door, worked her mouth up and down a couple of times, then simply shook her head and left, softly shutting the door behind her.

Mike turned off the few remaining lights, then stood for a moment scanning the skyline out the window next to Fran's desk. He'd finally let both his grandfather and Zoe's sisters in on his subterfuge, which all parties enthusiastically endorsed. What Zoe might say, however...

He loved her. It was that simple. And he still didn't know how all the pieces would fit. But if he let her drift out of his life without at least *trying*...

He'd never forgive himself.

He rubbed his hand over his face. Of all the harebrained things he'd ever done in his life—including some frathouse pranks he'd just as soon not remember—this was the most harebrained. All he had going for him was the element of surprise.

And the hope that he could talk faster than Zoe could slam a door in his face.

Her mother had called three times since five o'clock. It had gotten to the point where Zoe recognized her ring.

"No, Ma, I'm not wearing the black velvet. Casual, he said... Yeah, that's right. *I* told *him* Caraveggio's..." One hand streaked through her bangs. "Because it's my favorite restaurant, that's why... I told you, I didn't think it would be a long evening. He sounded like he had a cold or something when he called... Yes, Ma, I'll be nice. Good*bye,* Ma," she said, leaning down with the phone, slamming the receiver into the cradle the second her mother took a breath.

Sheesh, as Margi would say.

The kitchen clock said 7:10. So he was ten minutes late already. Zoe dashed back to her room, checked herself in the cheval mirror in the corner. Yeah, this would be fine. Her favorite hunter green chenille tunic over matching leggings, with her black suede skimmers. She ran a comb through her loose hair, threw on a string of amber beads Brianna had given her last Christmas, spritzed on some perfume.

She stopped dead, staring at herself in the mirror.

She was nervous. Maybe even...excited?

Naaah.

The doorbell rang. She jumped, squealed, raced down the curved staircase and out to the front door, stopped and collected herself. Anticipating. Tall…gorgeous…killer smile, Margi had said. Pecs to die for, had been Vanessa's contribution.

Okay, she thought, let's be realistic. Even if he's a loser, at least he'll be a gorgeous loser. Things could be worse.

Through the pebbled glass, hazed by the front porch light, she could see the *tall* part of the description was right on.

"Don't get yourself in a state," she muttered. "It's just a blind date. Not as if it's—" She opened the door and jumped a foot, her hand to her throat.

Flowers. Hundreds of them, it seemed, practically spilling out of his arms. Lilies and glads and all sorts of wonderful blossoms she didn't even recognize.

What a waste.

"What the hell are *you* doing here?"

He smiled. Yeah, *his* smile was nothing to sneeze at, either.

"Hoping you'll hear me out," he said. "Maybe…have dinner with me, give a chance to—"

"As it happens," she interrupted him, "I'm not available." Knuckling one hand into her hip, she returned his smile. Smug. Triumphant. Determined not to let him know that her heart was flitting around in her chest like a looped moth. Contrition sat well on his features, she mused.

"I have a date this evening." *Or will have,* she thought, *if the turkey ever shows up*. She angled her wrist slightly to sneak a glance at her watch. Twenty minutes late already. Not a good sign.

"Oh." His face collapsed into a frown. "Yeah, I should have known better than to just drop in. But I figured you probably wouldn't answer my phone calls—"

She pulled herself up a little straighter. All the way to fivefoot-one. "You figured right."

"And the salon isn't exactly the place to talk, either."

"Why would I want to talk?" She crossed her arms and leaned against the doorjamb. Watching him standing there holding all those flowers. Making him suffer. It was the least she could do. Upstairs, the phone rang.

"All right, then…if I have to say my piece here, I will.… Don't you need to get that?"

"It's probably just my mother," she said with a quick shrug. "And I've already talked to her three times. Since I'm not supposed to be here anyway, the machine can get it." The ringing stopped, only to start up again.

She saw him flick a glance over her head, toward the stairs. Reflex, she supposed. Those business types were all the same. If a phone rang, it was supposed to be answered. Immediately.

His eyes met hers again. He tried to hand her the flowers. "These are for you."

"And what does it mean if I accept them?"

The machine picked up; she heard her own voice drift down the stairs.

"That you like flowers?" He lowered them, his face concerned. "You do *like* them, don't you?"

She sighed. "I don't kill them on purpose, if that's what you mean." Against her better judgment, she reached out and touched a fragile white lily, speckled with red. "And these are very pretty—"

"Zoe?" came Margi's panicked voice on the machine. Zoe whipped around—if she could hear Margi all the way down here, she must be yelling. Which meant something was wrong—

"Oh, God, Zo—please be there, please, please—"

Zoe streaked up the stairs, yanking up the phone so fast, the base fell to the floor. "What, honey? I'm here, I'm here—"

"My water broke! And you know what the doctor said about the fire in my crotch? How about ten alarms?"

"Oh, God. Oh, damn. Oh…ohmigod! You're in labor!"

Mike was beside her, still hanging on to the flowers. "Is it your sister?"

She nodded, frantic and excited and scared to death. "Where's Scott?"

Now her sister's voice was inexplicably steady. "Creep had

a sudden weekend trip. We thought, since it was two weeks yet, we'd be okay.''

''It *is* okay,'' Zoe insisted, patting the air in front of her, trying to calm down. ''So where is he?''

''About two hours away. When the contractions started, I left a message at his motel....''

''When they *started?*'' Zoe practically shrieked. ''And how long ago was that, if you don't mind my asking?''

''About five,'' Margi said in a tiny voice. ''I was just so sure it was false labor again, but I left the message for Scott...well, just in case, you know?''

Zoe sighed. ''And did you call Mom and Dad?''

''I tried a few minutes ago. But they must have gone out to dinner.'' Zoe stared at the phone in disbelief. She'd just talked to the woman twenty minutes ago. *Now* she goes out.

''And I don't know where Van and Harry are, either. I've left messages on half the freakin' answering machines in Atlanta, it seems. So it looks like you're the designated driver, honey. *Ooooh...!*''

Margi's wail ended in a word Zoe didn't even know Margi knew.

On the other end of the line, her sister panted through the contraction, took a cleansing breath at the end. Wow—just like in the prenatal classes. ''Marg, honey,'' she asked when she figured her sister would hear her, ''how far apart are the contractions?''

''Th-three minutes. And strong.''

''*Three minutes?* Already? I thought this was your first baby?''

''Ha-ha. Which reminds me. I forgot to tell you, when I went in for my exam yesterday, the doctor said all those Braxton-Hicks had already dilated me to three centimeters.''

It took less than a second to figure this one out. ''So you're telling me you only have seven to go?''

''I'm telling you,'' Margi said with the unreasonable calmness of a woman about to give birth, ''if you don't get your butt over here and get me to the hospital like *yesterday,* I'm gonna have to squat right here in my living room and deliver this kid myself. And for some reason, I'm not really in the mood...oh, *God!*"

"We'll be right there, honey."

She dropped the phone—Mike had picked the base up off the floor—then ran to the kitchen and yanked her car keys off the hook, grabbing her tote bag as she flew to the front door.

"Forget it, Zo. You're not driving."

She whipped around to find him standing at the kitchen sink, which he'd filled with water so he could finally dump the flowers. "What, you expect me to walk?"

"I'll drive, Zo. You'll get us killed. I'll go start the car while you, uh, leave a note for your...date."

"Ohmigod—Michael." She met his puzzled expression with a quick shake of her head. "No, no...not *you*, Michael. *Him*, Michael. My date. I forgot..." She checked the clock over the mantel. Seven-thirty. "The hell with him," she said with a flick of her hands. "If he's this late, he gets what he deserves. Come on."

Hitching her purse strap onto her shoulder, she started back out the door, only to feel herself jerked back into the apartment and against Mike's solid chest, her purse swinging around and banging into his back. Whatever she was going to say was forgotten as he lifted her off her feet, crushing his mouth to hers in a kiss clearly designed to obliterate any arguments or reasons or objections she might have had as to why he should even be here, let alone kiss her. Her sister was in labor, she thought over the blood pounding in her head. She needed to get to her. Now. Immediately. And while all these urgent thoughts pranced through her brain, she entwined her arms around his neck and kissed him back, as thoroughly as she knew how.

They were both panting when they finally broke the suction. Slowly, gently, he lowered her back to earth, mentally as well as physically.

"Were you pretending that time?" he asked, his breath still warming her lips.

She shook her head. "You?"

His smile sent tingles all the way out to the satin bows on her skimmers. "What do you think?"

"I think…we have some serious talking to do—*later*."

Then she grabbed his hand and yanked him out the door.

11

——◆——

Just goes to show, Mike thought as he drove Zoe to her sister's house, the more you plan, the more likely fate is to rip things out of your hands and say, "No, stupid—you're gonna do it my *way.*"

If only fate would be so kind as to supply a new script when it pulled one of these numbers, life would be so much easier.

He'd been ready to plead, if necessary, for her to hear him out. To give him a chance to convince her that he'd gladly reorder his life to make room for her. Because life without her would be too empty to contemplate, even if he worked eighteen hours a day. Without her it would all be pointless.

Instead he'd kissed her. Thrown himself at her without giving her two seconds to figure out what, if anything, was going on. Without letting her know what he was thinking.

Without telling her he loved her. Needed her, wanted her, cherished her. He'd fully intended to tell her all that, somewhere close to the beginning of the conversation. Where had all the words gone? Guess fate had other ideas about that, too.

Okay, she'd kissed him back—boy, had she kissed him back!—but now, inexplicably, she wasn't even talking to him.

Oh, brother.

Zoe was out of the car and up her sister's front steps before he'd even shut off the engine. He barely had time to open the back door when Zoe ushered a panting Margi out of the house, her sister's suitcase clutched in her right hand. He thought

Margi was walking strangely, even for a woman in the advanced stages of pregnancy. Then he noticed she had wadded a towel between her legs.

"She's still leaking," Zoe explained without his asking, guiding Margi onto the back seat.

"Spurting, if you really want to know," she said.

He really didn't.

"Are you going to ride back there with her?" he asked Zoe, which earned him a classic *And what planet are you from?* look. "Just asking. Okay…" he said, settling back behind the wheel. "Where are we going?"

Margi had just enough time and breath between contractions to tell him *exactly* the route to get to the hospital. "We timed it. If you made all the green lights, it takes exactly nine minutes."

They hit every red light in Druid Hills. Including some that Mike swore had never been there before.

Zoe did some swearing of her own. Such a sweet woman he'd fallen in love with, he mused. "What the hell are you doing, Michael? The woman's about to have a baby, for God's sake!"

He caught her panicked face in the rearview mirror. "Would you rather I ran a red light and we get creamed by an oncoming car?" he calmly asked. "Then, providing we lived, of course, we would all have reason to go to the hospital."

She stuck her tongue out at him. But she didn't say another word.

About twenty blocks from the hospital, he asked, "How far apart—?"

"They're coming right on top of each other now," Zoe said. He could hear how valiantly she was fighting to keep her voice level.

Margi, however, seemed perfectly calm. In agony, but calm. Suddenly her breathing pattern changed, and she began to huff and wheeze in short, sharp, vicious bursts of air.

"Ohmigod, she's gone into transition," Zoe said, a decibel

or two higher than her normal voice. Then, out of the blue, she asked Mike, "Do you know what that is?"

"As a matter of fact, one of my accounts is a company that specializes in prenatal education. They had a film—"

"Okay, okay. A simple *yes* would have been fine."

He pulled into the hospital parking lot. Again, Zoe sprang into action before he could even think about what came next, let alone act on it. Even one step removed from hysteria, he realized, she was a model of efficiency. He was beginning to understand why Brianna would kill for this woman.

And beginning to understand even more why *he* would.

About twenty feet from the hospital entrance, Margi came to a dead halt and screamed. Just *screamed*. An ear-splitting, primal wail that instantly brought a dozen people streaking out of the hospital toward them.

"She's in labor," Zoe said.

"Transition," Mike added, feeling…useless.

Now they had to run to keep up with the orderly sprinting ahead with Margi—who was no longer the least bit calm—in a wheelchair. She was swallowed into the bowels of the maternity wing as Zoe and Mike shoved people aside at the admissions desk. Mike apologized. Zoe didn't.

Rattling like a printer, Zoe efficiently spit out all the pertinent information to the beleaguered nurse at the desk. "She's preregistered but wasn't due for two weeks yet. Is her doctor here yet? Where did you put Margi? She wants me in there with her—I'm her secondary coach, and the father—"

"Are you Mrs. Lee's family?" someone asked behind them, making them both jump.

"I'm her sister," Zoe asked. "Who the hell are you?"

Mike put his hand at the small of her back. "She gets a little…obstreperous under pressure."

"Don't we all?" the young—far too young to be a doctor—man replied mildly. Pale blue eyes twinkled like diamonds in a smooth face lit with an engaging—and somewhat calming—smile. "Well, I've just checked Mrs. Lee, and she's just about fully dilated, so I've put her right into the birthing room. Why don't you two follow Miss Johnson here—'' he gestured toward a grinning African-American woman ''—and get into scrubs, and…I guess I meet you there?''

''But I'm not—'' Mike started to say.

But Zoe had grabbed his hand and started down the hall after the young man, clearly determined that hell would freeze over before she let go.

Taking Zoe's sister to the hospital was one thing, Mike thought, wondering how on earth he managed to get himself in these things. Being present at the birth was something else again. An image of Butterfly McQueen in *Gone With the Wind,* declaring ''I don't know nothing 'bout birthin' no babies!'' kept whizzing through his brain.

He glanced over at the woman he loved…and realized the woman he loved was likely to keep getting him into ''these things'' for the rest of his life.

With a sigh, he stuck the stupid little blue cap they gave him on his head and followed Zoe and the nurse back down the hall and into Margi's birthing room.

Margi—understandably preoccupied—hadn't yet said anything, he realized. Maybe she assumed that Zoe already knew that he and the ''other'' Michael were the same person, that he'd already explained everything, that Zoe had forgiven him, that everything was hunky-dory.

And maybe not.

It was like being in a room with a ticking time bomb.

He found himself slinking along the wall, inching closer to the door. Zoe was so into her taking-charge role that she'd never notice if he left, he was sure. Right now, her energies were firmly focused on this *child* who seemed to be actually considering delivering her sister's baby.

As the man placidly made preparations for the birth, Zoe was right in his face, scrappy and fearless. ''Excuse me…but since when do they let med students deliver unattended?''

Clearly unfazed by her remark, the young doctor's mouth curved into a gentle smile as he studied the monitor. ''Haven't been a med student for more than fifteen years.'' He held out his hand. ''Joshua Grady, M.D. Resident OB on duty tonight.''

''Oh,'' Zoe said, meekly returning the handshake. ''Sorry.''

''Happens all the time. I'm used to it.''

''But where's Dr. Steinberg?''

''She's on her way, but I *don't* think she's gonna make it, by the looks of things.''

''That's ridiculous,'' Zoe said, eyeing her sister. ''This is her first baby.''

''Tell the baby that,'' Dr. Grady said with a grin. ''Okay, Mrs. Lee. Feel like pushing yet?''

Margi shook her head.

''Don't worry. You will. Dad?'' The doctor twisted around, found Mike. ''You know,'' he said, scratching behind his ear, ''I think you might be of more help to your wife up here?''

''My husband—'' Margi said, but was cut off by another contraction, even as she glared at her sister.

Now what? Mike wondered.

Zoe turned imploring eyes to him. She was scared, he realized. And wanted his help.

It wasn't exactly the most traditional of way of hearing the words, ''I love you.'' But then, this was Zoe.

As Mike hesitantly came to stand on Margi's other side, Zoe leaned close to her sister, taking her hand. She glanced up at Mike, then seemed to say to both of them, ''Sorry. Reflex action. Do you mind?''

Margi had maybe fifteen seconds before the next contraction. ''Honey, the Atlanta Braves could have batting practice in here and I wouldn't give a damn right now.'' Then she grinned. In transition, soaking wet with perspiration, about to give birth, her sister was grinning as if she'd just won a race. ''So, how do you like David Wu's grandson?''

In spite of the heat in the room, Mike felt his skin go stone-cold.

Zoe expelled an indignant sigh. ''The creep never showed up. I should have known.''

Mike saw confusion flit across Margi's features as she

looked from Zoe to Mike and back again. "What are you talking about, didn't show up? Oh! Oh!" Her face screwed up, but she managed to get out, "Who the hell do you think that is about to watch me give...oh my *Gooooood!* I want to push, I want to push, I want to *puuuuuush!*"

Over her sister's wracked, panting form as they tilted her forward so she could push, Mike met a pair of the angriest eyes he'd ever seen. Oh, hell—what was he supposed to do *now?*

So, stupidly, he tried a smile.

"You," Zoe spat across the bed, "are dead meat."

"Good girl," the doctor said to Margi, either oblivious to or ignoring the brawl about to erupt a few feet away. "This ain't gonna take long at all," he said with a contented sigh as he settled back, waiting for the next contraction. "It never ceases to amaze me, but the little ones often have the easiest time of it. The baby's not overly large, either, so...okay, folks—here we go again."

Margi pushed, Zoe fumed, Mike wished he was dead.

"You *knew!*" she seethed. "All this time, you *knew.*"

The hospital door burst open, and a blob of blue with wire-rimmed glasses and a goofy, half-panicked look on his face streaked to Margi's side, knocking Mike out of the way. Scott Lee clasped his wife's hand to his mouth, then kissed her, hard. "I was so scared I wasn't going to make it," he whispered, brushing her damp hair off her forehead.

"Who—?" Dr. Grady asked.

"The father!" chorused at least four people.

The doctor looked at each one in turn, shrugged, then got back to business.

"I knew you'd get here. I knew it," Margi said to Scott, for the moment focused on nothing but her husband's face. "We're going to have a baby, Scotty," she said, and then gasped with the power of the next contraction.

With strength and tenderness and an intuitive need to help his mate birth their baby, the slim, bespectacled man slipped an arm around Margi's shoulders and gently pushed her forward, whispering words of encouragement in her ear, his temple pressed against hers.

There was no reason for Mike to stay. He was a decided fifth—if not sixth or seventh—wheel to this private event. Yet something kept him in the room, almost as if some strange force surrounding the birth process had ensnared him, unwilling to let him go until he'd seen the completion of the miracle.

This was love, he thought, in all its forms, in one spot. Man for woman, parent for child, sister for sister—the endless cycle of family that kept the world from falling apart.

As the birth grew nearer, he was sucked into the intensity and passion of the moment. The film he'd watched was nothing compared with the live performance, that was for sure. And somewhere along the line, his grandmother's face sprang to mind. Puzzled, he tried to focus on the image, almost as if she was literally in the room with him. She was smiling, and nodding, as if in approval. Then he heard her say, not so much in his head as in his heart, "A sacrifice made for love isn't a sacrifice, but a blessing. There is no loss, or pain, or dishonor in such a sacrifice. I was happy, Michael. Believe that…. I was happy."

Zoe stood on the opposite side of the bed, clutching her sister's hand, her face glowing with excitement and anticipation as Margi's labor sped up. She suddenly looked over to him, for just a second, as if someone had tapped her on the shoulder. But before he could meet her eyes, Margi leaned forward into a push that could have shifted Mount Everest, taking Zoe's attention with her.

Tears sprang to Zoe's eyes at the sight of Scott calmly coaching his shrieking wife through the last few minutes of her labor, as the baby fought its way into the world. Her own hand was nearly crushed from Margi's death grip, as the force of the birth overtook and obliterated everything else in the room. Nothing existed, for those few minutes, save the power and urgency of new life appearing.

Somewhere, though, in the back of Zoe's mind, stung the

hurt of having been tricked and manipulated and played for a fool. Despite the drama unfolding three feet away, in spite of Margi's howls as the baby moved down and the doctor's encouraging hurrahs—the man must've been a sports coach, she thought absently—and Scott's exuberant cries of delight when the baby's black-haired head crowned, the thought that Mike hadn't had the guts to simply confront her, without resorting to some adolescent subterfuge, cut her to the quick.

Or so she wanted to believe. Suddenly, something impelled her to glance over at him where he stood a careful few feet away, and she saw the expression of wonder—and hope—on his face.

And every trace of anger vanished.

After all, hadn't she tricked him, too, in a way, dragging him in here because she'd been afraid to face this alone? And even though she knew this wasn't exactly where he'd wanted to be, he'd gone along with her.

The man had been willing to witness the birth of a child not even related to him, for no other reason than she needed him with her.

Margie's next scream—a guttural sound that brought the words, "This is it, folks!" from the doctor's lips—recaptured her attention in time to witness the baby sliding out into the doctor's latexed hands. Like an engine needing a few warm-up gurgles before kicking in, the tiny boy scrunched up his red face, sputtered for a second, then broke forth into a lusty, gorgeous, ear-piercing wail.

"No need to clear this one's passages, folks," Dr. Grady said with a laugh as the nurse quickly wrapped the infant in a receiving blanket and lay him on Margi's stomach. "Your son is gorgeous," the doctor said softly, then grinned at the slightly delirious couple. "You done good, Mom."

Zoe took a deep breath and glanced over at Mike. He was leaning against the wall with one hand covering his mouth. His eyes, when he lifted them to Zoe, were shimmering with tears.

If she never saw Mike Kwan again after tonight, came the

kick-to-the-gut thought, she would love him for the rest of her life.

When Scott lowered the bundled-up baby into Zoe's arms, she nearly whimpered with how beautiful he was. Already, his tiny fists were pummeling at the world, his head a tiny black bowling ball, the fontanel softly, strongly beating. Zoe touched the spot, amazed, and the baby opened his eyes, just for a second, before, preceded by a yawn far too wide for such a tiny thing, he drifted back to sleep.

"Oh, wow—he yawned," she whispered, and heard Margi snigger a few feet away.

"Yeah. I hear they eat and poop pretty well, too," she said, holding out her arms. "Time's up, Auntie. Give me my baby."

Reluctantly—so much it hurt—she relinquished her new nephew to his mother's arms, only to feel Mike's slide around her shoulders. "Come on, *Auntie*. Let's give the new family a minute to themselves," he murmured into her hair, then led her out of the room.

Her parents and Vanessa and Harry all leapt up out of their seats, no one the least perturbed or even curious that Zoe had just walked out of her sister's delivery room in the arms of some man they'd never met. Oh, yeah, she remembered—they *had* met Mike. Still…

"Well?" her mother said, beaming. "What'd we get?"

"A boy," Zoe said, hearing the awe in her voice. "A gorgeous, fat, sassy little boy with this mop of black hair…." She stopped, pressing her fingers to her lips, as her eyes swam again.

"What is it?" her father asked, taking her hand. Behind his glasses, his eyes danced with concern. "Nothing went wrong, did it?"

"What?" Perplexed, she stared at her father through a wall of saltwater. "Oh! No, no, no—everything went beautifully. He's perfect, and Margi's fine. It's just…" She shook her head.

Her mother was there, her soft, slender hand on her cheek. "I know" was all she said. "I know."

"Okay, folks," the delivery nurse called from Margi's doorway. "There's one feisty little dude in here who wants to meet the rest of his family, so you better hop to, now."

She didn't have to ask twice. They had vanished into the room before she'd finished the invitation.

Zoe felt Mike leading her to a pair of empty waiting room chairs, where they both sank as if someone had pulled the pins out from their knees. He still had his arm around her; without even a murmur of protest, she let him guide her head against his shoulder.

"Well, lady," he whispered into her hair. "You sure know how to show a guy a good time. All I'd had in mind was linguine with white clam sauce."

She looked up at him, puzzled for a second, then remembered. "Oh, right. It was you who made the reservation at Caraveggio's. Not that I would have gone—"

"No," he said, shifting nervously under her head. "Will you ever forgive me for that? I just couldn't think of anything else to do, and I'm afraid I'm not very good at any of this—"

Barely managing a chuckle, she lay her hand on his chest, smiling when he took it in his hand and kissed her palm.

"Actually," she said softly, "you're very good at this. And, eventually, I suppose I'll forgive you. Since you leave me no choice."

She heard unmistakable relief in his sigh. Then "How're you doing?"

"Ask me when the adrenaline returns to normal."

"Know what you mean." She felt his lips graze the top of her head and closed her eyes to shut out everything but that. "So…you think you might want one of those yourself someday?"

Her eyes popped open. She reared back to let herself float in that smile. She *did*, she realized. More than anything in the world at that moment, she wanted to have a baby. And, after the last couple of hours, she knew damn well what that meant, in Technicolor detail.

"Yes," she said, locking their gazes.

"Do you think, then…" For a moment, he studied their interlocked hands. Then focused once again on her face. "You think…you might like to have one with me?"

Now she sat bolt upright, her heart ramming so hard in her chest, it hurt. "What are you saying, Michael Kwan?"

He scratched his head, and the look on his face was priceless. With a sound somewhere between a snort and a laugh, he said, mostly to himself, "This is hardly the way I'd ever envisioned this happening, in some fluorescent-lit waiting room, wearing scrubs. But somehow it seems to fit—"

To her shock, he got down on one knee, taking her hands in his. She sensed all other activity in the waiting room come to a halt, all noise drown in a collective, expectant hush. "I should have told you then, in New York, that I'd never been pretending. You grabbed my heart from the moment I saw you, made me sit up and take notice. Made me realize that something had been missing from my life I didn't even realize *was* missing. You make me feel alive, Zoe. And needed. And you've made me realize what's really important. And—"

"Stop," she said, placing one hand on his lips.

Fear and panic and utter disappointment streaked across his handsome face. "Stop?" he choked out.

"If you say anything more, I won't be able to remember it. And God *knows* I want to remember every single word of this for the rest of my life."

"You're crying?" Smiling now, he reached up and smoothed a tear off her cheek.

"Ohhh," she exhaled, "I have a feeling you ain't seen nothin' yet."

"Okay. I'll stop. After just one more sentence."

She nodded. And realized, to her amazement, she was quivering.

"Will you marry me, Zoe Chan? Will you work with me

to sort out our complicated, busy lives enough to make room for each other? To raise a family and make a home together?''

She cocked her head. "That was three sentences. Questions, if you want to get technical.''

He pulled himself up to take her face in his hands. "You're impossible, you know that?''

"Yep. You sure you want my answer?''

"Preferably before my knees give out, yes.''

She giggled and threaded her arms around his neck. "Yes, Michael Kwan,'' she whispered. "I want to marry you, to mesh my life with yours, to make a home and children with you. You, too, made me realize what I'd been missing. And then had the guts to make an idiot of yourself and show up on my doorstep, pretending to be yourself. Now I ask you— what girl in her right mind could resist that?''

He grinned. "So...this means you aren't wigged out from the birth or anything?''

"Nope.''

"That's a profound—'' he struggled up off his knees and landed a trifle clumsily in the chair "—relief. 'Cause ten years down the road, I'm not letting you plead temporary insanity.''

"Mm...'' She snuggled against his shoulder. "Not to worry.''

They sat in silence for several minutes, as oblivious to the goings-on around them as if they were the only two people in the room. Then, with a gentle squeeze to her shoulder, Mike said, "I remember a Chinese proverb my grandfather told me once, years ago. 'Because I live by chance, I love by choice.' Took me all this time to figure out what that meant.''

Lifting her head, Zoe smiled into his eyes. "Your grandfather,'' she said, "is a very wise man.''

"Lord, don't tell him that. You'll never hear the end of it.''

She laughed. "Point taken. But you know...'' She settled her head once again where she could hear his heart, strong and loving. "This just may make me change my mind about Chinese food.''

Mike chuckled. "I only know one thing that would make the old man happier."

Looking into his eyes, she said, "And what's that?"

He smiled, kissed her on the nose. "Hearing that he was right about you."

Epilogue

The following January

The Golden Dragon was closed to the public the night of David Wu's grandson's wedding. Even so, there were more people than tables. Not that anyone cared. Outside, rain occasionally mixed with biting sleet slashed across the storefront windows. No one cared about that, either.

The old man's face hurt from grinning so widely, from accepting congratulations from old friends and relatives, from accepting compliments on his food. He had hired ten cooks—including one of Vittorio Caraveggio's because Mike had told him that his bride had a thing for shrimp scampi—for this all-important wedding banquet, and they had all been kept more than busy since five that afternoon. The banquet was his wedding present to his youngest grandson, who had had the good sense, and graciousness, to accept. There was hope for the boy yet, he mused.

Eyes that had seen a hundred weddings, including those of three children and five grandchildren, scanned the restaurant, purposeful and content.

This is what life was meant to be. People coming together to celebrate the joyous passages of life. That oneness, he reflected as he thought of his wife of nearly sixty years, now gone three, made the sorrowful passages easier to bear.

His three children, their spouses and children and children's children, were all there, faces wreathed in smiles, voices ringing with laughter and best wishes. There were friends old to him, and friends he had yet to meet.

And, in the center of it all, the bridal couple, so much in love they would have glowed without the benefit of the hundreds of parchment lanterns hung from the ceiling.

This Zoe Chan was an exquisite beauty, in her simple satin wedding gown and airy veil, trios of tiny diamonds sparkling in her ears. He chuckled. Three holes in each ear? Then he shrugged his aching shoulders. Oh, why not? On her, it worked, so what was the big deal?

And Michael, handsome and proud and strong in his tuxedo, barely able to take his eyes off his bride. He raised a toast, his arm possessively encircling his new wife's tiny waist. In the back of the restaurant, David Wu raised a glass of champagne in return. No one would see it, but he would know he'd joined in.

"To choices!" Michael called out, then looked at Zoe. "And to the wisdom to know which ones to make."

And in the din of laughter and wishes for happiness that followed, David Wu felt, in his heart, his wife's blessing.

* * * * *

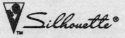

Take 2 bestselling love stories FREE

Plus get a FREE surprise gift!

Special Limited-Time Offer

Mail to Silhouette Reader Service™

3010 Walden Avenue
P.O. Box 1867
Buffalo, N.Y. 14269-1867

YES! Please send me 2 free Silhouette Yours Truly™ novels and my free surprise gift. Then send me 4 brand-new novels every other month, which I will receive months before they appear in bookstores. Bill me at the low price of $2.90 each plus 25¢ delivery and applicable sales tax, if any.* That's the complete price, and a saving of over 10% off the cover prices—quite a bargain! I understand that accepting the books and gift places me under no obligation ever to buy any books. I can always return a shipment and cancel at any time. Even if I never buy another book from Silhouette, the 2 free books and the surprise gift are mine to keep forever.

201 SEN CH72

Name	(PLEASE PRINT)	
Address	Apt. No.	
City	State	Zip

This offer is limited to one order per household and not valid to present Silhouette Yours Truly™ subscribers. *Terms and prices are subject to change without notice. Sales tax applicable in N.Y.

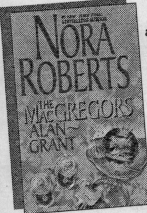

Sneak Previews of March titles from Yours Truly™:

A MATCH FOR MORGAN
The Cutlers of the Shady Lady Ranch
by Marie Ferrarella

Morgan Cutler had thought her lifelong desire for
Wyatt McCall was long gone—until she discovered
he was single again. Troubled by the feelings he aroused in
her, Morgan struggled to keep him out of her thoughts.
But, with love and marriage in the air at the Shady Lady
Ranch, she secretly hoped it was only a matter of time
before this girl-next-door became his bride-to-be.

DID YOU SAY *BABY?!*
by Lynn Miller

When beautiful Rebecca Chandler showed up on his
Texas ranch, JD McCoy's calm life was suddenly
turned upside down. In her hands was his runaway sister's
baby…that *he* was supposed to take care of? Taking
pity on his lack of fatherhood know-how, Rebecca
stuck around to help the sexy stranger get used to his new-
found role. But when the mother surprisingly reappeared,
Rebecca's decision to leave made JD
realize just how much he felt for this woman—
and what he would do to hold on to her.